WISPA

WISPA

TIM PARKER

urlink
PRINT & MEDIA

WISPA

1603 Capitol Ave., Suite 310 Cheyenne, Wyoming USA 82001
1-888-980-6523 | admin@urlinkpublishing.com

URLink Print and Media is committed to excellence in the publishing industry.

Published in the United States of America

ISBN 978-1-64367-658-6 (Paperback)
ISBN 978-1-64367-659-3 (Digital)

31.07.19

This book is dedicated to:
NATALIE 1943 - 2019

It's been nineteen years since our school reunion:

Brian sang, "It started over coffee . . ."
But perhaps some things are just meant to be.

It almost happened just like that with us.
I wondered if I just fell off a bus.

Figured I would go and have a few beers.
Nothing expected after forty years.

As singles again we meet for the first time.
Never met when I barely had a dime.

Prologue

WISPA (New England pronunciation of whisper) is based on actual terrorist threats to municipal water supplies for millions of people since 9/11. In more recent years, trespassers were apprehended on government property in Massachusetts, New York and Canada.

Because of their unique skills, the principle characters in the book were enlisted to go undercover for the United States Government where they often needed to whisper. Eventually they became targets of terrorists and had to go into hiding while helping to make the United States safer from their threats.

My thanks go out to the Bay Path University Writers' Group for their valuable feedback. Inputs from my brother Jerry and sister Sue were very helpful as well. I thank them for their patience in rereading the manuscript several times as it evolved. Special thanks and a halo should be awarded to Natalie for her tolerance and support throughout the whole composition process.

Scenes and locations may sound familiar to residents of western Massachusetts, but many were modified, moved or subjected to name changes.

Comments on the book are welcomed at: ParkerWare@aol.com

Other books by Tim Parker:

Peter Pickering, a British businessman working undercover for the CIA, disappeared in Switzerland. His wife, Monique hired detective Tom Powers to find Peter when he failed to meet her in Amsterdam after a Zurich business trip. Pickering, a distributor of components for durable goods, was recruited to help stop the drain of United States technology for use in weapons by terrorists and rogue nations.

Ultimately, Peter turned up with amnesia as a John Doe left for dead in Germany. Pickering's journal was missing, which may have contained clues about who attacked him and why. Tom was shot by an intruder at the client's home in the Berkshires protecting C.I.A. agent Joan Walters.

The investigators traveled to Europe for answers but encountered spies who killed one of Peter's Zurich customers and ransacked his office. Tom's life was saved by the young agent who took down one of the spies and captured the other seeking American technology secrets.

Tom and Joan then became more than partners working in Switzerland to stop the flow of arms to terrorists.

Soon to be released:

TOUCH DOWN

or

AEROSpace MEMOIR

This book describes how I helped build space suits and accessories fifty years ago to land NASA Apollo 11 astronauts on the moon in July 1969 and return safely.

1

Why didn't I listen to that little voice inside my head that said, *Don't go to your twentieth college reunion. You've got too many things on your desk that absolutely have to be done by the end of the weekend.* I should have known returning to Dana University in Irving after all these years was a bad idea. It took me so long to get over Michael and put him out of my head. Now all those memories I thought were comfortably buried have been dredged back to the surface again by this trip back in time.

Maybe I should have listened when Michael proposed to me back in college, but no. I insisted my career must come first. Long before marriage and certainly way before contemplating children. Once I was established in the business world with enough experience under my belt and insider knowledge on how to play company politics to get above the glass ceiling, *then…*

I just figured I'd been so busy becoming indispensable in my job; I didn't have time for the fifth or tenth reunions. What harm could it do now to catch up with old friends for a change of pace? I certainly haven't had time for male or female friends for years. There was always another meeting to prepare for. Another business trip that no one else could take and produce the same results I could.

I've always said, "If you don't think you're good, nobody else will, and I'm one of the best traders on Wall Street." At least that's what I would tell myself. I'll be darned if I'm ever accused of sleeping my way to the top. They may call me driven behind my back, but I always got where I wanted to go on my own merits, and they knew for sure I had earned my position.

When I think back to all the nights I had curled up on the sofa with Profit and Loss (P&L) statements and balance sheets instead of being with someone who loved me... Too many times I had been so lonely that I cried myself to sleep when I couldn't concentrate on preparing for yet another all-important staff meeting the first thing in the morning.

I guess what brought this all to a boil was arriving for the reunion late in the day on campus as the sun just started to set in a field of brilliant reds and yellows. I saw a student in silhouette. He was under the very ivy-covered, brick archway with the wrought iron gates where Michael and I first met. His broad shoulders and erect posture even reminded me of Michael.

I can remember meeting Michael for the first time only too well. I was a freshman, walking to English class when I heard the timbre in his voice behind me resonating off the brick walls of the courtyard. Even the echoes of his deep voice seemed to have echoes. Naturally, I wanted to keep my cool, so I stopped just long enough to peek over my shoulder with my compact case mirror. He was drop dead gorgeous! His little friend wasn't half bad either, but Michael could have posed for a statue of a Greek God and been a distraction at the unveiling.

Walking a few more steps to accentuate the clicking of my heels on the polished stone walkway and adding a little extra wiggle in my hips, I shifted the pile of books to my other arm. Naturally, I dropped the whole stack. Michael and Tom quickly surged ahead to aid the damsel in distress. I could have swooned looking up into those deep blue eyes, firmly set into the high cheekbones above the square jaw.

He introduced himself and his friend then convinced me to meet him for coffee at the Student Union after class. He didn't have to twist my arm. We talked forever about our tastes in music, books, courses, schedules, sports, and everything else. It was amazing how much we had in common. Before I left, he asked me to his fraternity party that weekend.

From that moment on we were inseparable. It seemed as though we were meant to be together and had a mad, passionate relationship. We just couldn't get enough of each other.

A little over a year later, he proposed when he was a junior, but I was only a sophomore. As difficult as it was, I told Michael no, because I wanted to focus on a career first before settling down. Michael tried his best to assure me I could have a successful career while being a wife and mother, but I felt otherwise. Although it broke my heart, thinking about what could have been, I tried to avoid him on campus after that.

I threw myself back into my studies, finished at the top of my class, and went on to complete my graduate studies in finance in record time. It's been "shoulder to the wheel" and "nose to the grindstone" ever since. I'd dedicated almost twenty years of my life to the Grady Trading Company, and what did I have to show for it other than an ocean of stock options and a golden parachute should I survive to retirement age?

I'm almost past the age to consider having a child, and I have no personal life. It was nice to be able to say I'm one of the youngest vice presidents in the financial world, but what good is that? I have enough income saved to live more than comfortably, but nobody to share it with. They really weren't kidding when they said it's lonely at the top.

Well, this was exactly what I was afraid of coming back to Dana University in Irving. Here I was regretting what I might have missed by postponing the start of a family for too long. I only wanted to loosen up this weekend and have a little fun for a change. I also need to get out of this power suit and stop talking to myself before I start to get answers.

The campus was well lit, but it was starting to get dark. I decided to walk over to see if the Kenwood Diner still made a great cup of coffee. I thought maybe it would perk me up after driving all day to get here from the city. I was starting to get a little drowsy.

Turning the corner, I was pleasantly surprised to find it was still there. The railcar diner always appeared to be a greasy spoon from the outside, yet the meals were great and reasonably priced back in the day.

It seemed to be pretty crowded in there. Maybe I could find a seat at the counter. I wish that kid hadn't held the door open for me like I was a little old lady, but I'm sure he was just trying to be polite. Jeez. They all looked so young. And we thought we were so grown up at that age. That one didn't even look like he was old enough to shave yet.

Inside the diner with the arched ceiling hadn't changed at all. I was sure that the "Breakfast served all day" sign and the daily specials blackboard, which listed the soup de jour, were both originals. I didn't think the hand printed menus in their clear plastic folders had changed either. It looked like the chrome-plated stools with the nicked red vinyl covers at the counter haven't been replaced. The mixture of all the smells of different foods cooking at the same time still overwhelmed the senses too.

I was in luck. There was an empty seat. The man on the next stool turned to face me. "Michael?" I said looking at a familiar yet somehow unfamiliar face. "What are you doing here? Oh, I'm so sorry. I thought you were someone else."

"You may have mistaken me for my cousin, Mike. People say we look enough alike to be brothers. I was saving a seat for him, but he must be running late. Since there doesn't appear to be any other places available, would you care to sit here?"

"Thank you. I'm Pam. I was only planning to stay long enough to have a cup of coffee. It was a difficult drive up from New York City today." I tossed my hair back and slanted my head to the side to get a better look at him as I sat down. Besides the dark hair, chiseled features, and intense blue eyes, he looked like he was tall enough to be a slightly older version of the Michael I knew in college. His tweed jacket with the suede leather patches on the elbows suggested he might work at the university. His loose tie and unbuttoned collar implied he'd had a hard day, yet he seemed congenial enough with his broad smile.

"Hi. I'm Jake. I live nearby. Mike said he would be passing through town on business and asked if I could meet him for a sandwich. Will you be meeting Mike or someone else here?" he said, raising those bushy eyebrows while furling his brow.

"No, I came for a class reunion at DUI, but the close resemblance to your cousin is amazing," I said with a smile, trying not to stare for too long.

"Coffee sounds like a great idea. Did you want anything with that? Maybe a piece of their famous apple pie?" Jake replied with an irresistible grin that lit up his face.

"Just black coffee please, Jake. I haven't been getting out of the office often enough to exercise lately, so I don't need any extra calories."

"You look like you're in pretty good shape to me, if you'll pardon me for saying so," Jake said as he tried to force himself to break eye contact. He was surprised a woman who would turn most men's heads, showed up in an off-campus diner. He thought to himself, *she could be a top fashion model in that smart business suit.*

"Thank you, but I have to watch what I eat or I get sluggish in those long afternoon business meetings," I said.

"I'll see if I can get the attention of the waitress. Miss, can we please have two black coffees over here when you get a chance? So, Pam, how do you know Mike?"

"We were a couple back in college, but it didn't work out."

"Oh, now I remember. You must be the one he said got away. Mike was pretty broken up about that for the longest time."

I interjected, "Someone recently told me that Michael is happily married, so I guess everything worked out well for him. Excuse me, but your pocket seems to be buzzing." I hope he didn't think I was staring down at his pants, but he seemed to be ignoring his phone. Jake stood up to extract the phone from his front pocket. Looking up at him, I was surprised. He appeared to be much taller than I had originally thought.

"It's a text from Mike. He's not coming after all because he's caught in a traffic jam. There's an empty table opening up by the window where it's probably quieter. Shall we take our coffees over there, so we can hear each other talk?" Jake asked.

"That sounds like a good idea. It just feels so nice to get out of the office and the city for a change."

"Here, let me move the coffees over to claim the table before someone else does."

"Thank you, Jake. What do you do for a living?"

"I'm a professor in the engineering department at DUI."

"Do you have a family? Is there a Mrs. Jake?" I asked sheepishly.

"No, I came close once with a high school sweetheart," Jake said.

"And that didn't work out?" I asked, almost sorry I brought up the subject.

"No, she didn't want to wait for me when I shipped overseas." After a long pause, Jake sipped his coffee and said, "Then I caught a bullet in my spine in Afghanistan."

"Oh, Jake, I'm so sorry to hear that. Did you recover fully from the wound?"

"No, but I met a nurse who spent extra time lifting my spirits to get me out of my funk." From pain of the memory, Jake dropped his head and was barely audible when he mumbled, "We were engaged to be married when my tour was up, but she was killed in a Humvee by a Taliban IED."

After I recoiled in shock, I reached across the table, put my hand on his as I looked into his sad eyes, and said, "Jake, that's terrible. What did you do then?"

"I went back to school on the GI Bill when I returned to the States," he said with resignation. "To make a long story short, I'm still single." After pausing a moment to regain his composure, his face brightened when he said, "Tell me about yourself."

After he shared his personal story, I wanted to reach out and give him a hug. Since he was so open with me, I said, "There's not a whole lot to tell. I landed a position on Wall Street after college. I worked my butt off until I was named vice president of finance for Grady Trading Company a couple of years ago."

"Boy, Pam, it sounds like your position wouldn't leave much time for family life," Jake said.

"I wouldn't know. I don't have a family. If I didn't push myself, someone would try to replace me. I had to work twice as hard as my male coworkers just to even the odds."

"What do you do in your free time?" Jake inquired.

"What's that?" I said. "I haven't taken a day off in the last five years. This trip was to be a break from the office routine. I figured I'd meet up with a few classmates, have a few laughs, and recharge my batteries with some downtime for a change.

"You said you drove up from the city today, Pam. Did you take time for lunch or dinner?"

"I didn't even eat breakfast. I left messages and ran out the door to try to beat the traffic, but that didn't work out. Everything crawled until I got past New Haven," I said.

"Well you can't possibly function without eating. Do you like Italian?"

"I do, Jake, but it doesn't always like me. I can't handle spicy."

"That's because the people in southern Italy and Mexico use too much pepper to help preserve the food, but it also covers up anything that's slightly tainted. I know of just the right place a few miles from here. It's called Luigi's. He came over from northern Italy where they cook differently. He eloped with a daughter of one of the Parker brothers without the family's blessing. She was promptly disowned, so they converted an old mansion for a restaurant. It's off the beaten path and looks like it was transported from the old country. They make a linguini al dente with a white clam sauce that's magnifico."

"That sounds delightful, Jake, but I hardly know you, and my car might get towed from the campus parking lot," I said.

"Pam, if you know Mike, then we're practically family, and you have to eat something anyway. I'll call the campus police to have them keep an eye on your car. I'm parked across the street. I hope you can get up in the cab of a full sized pickup truck in that skirt," Jake said as he left cash for the coffees and a tip.

"That probably won't be a problem if you give me a hand. What do you need a pickup for on campus, Jake?" I asked.

"My back. I still have bullet fragments in my spine that couldn't be removed safely. The seat in a full sized Chevy truck is contoured and elevated to fit someone my size. The average height for an American is only 5'6". To meet the EPA fuel economy requirements, cars and small trucks need a low profile, but they're not big enough for me," Jake answered.

"You sure sound like an engineer. Does that cause you a lot of pain?" I asked.

"Not if I try to ignore it. I see an osteopath almost every week. She uses acupressure and manipulation to relieve the swelling. I also do a special regimen of exercises that help strengthen my core.

It's the white truck right there. It doesn't have automated locks, so I'll open your side with the key. Here, let me help you up." Jake said when he lifted me off the ground as if I was as light as a feather.

"Jake, be careful of your back."

"I'm not that fragile, Pam. I can lift something my own weight if I tackle it straight on. It's turning and twisting that gives me grief."

"Next time I can do some of the lifting when I get up into the cab. I'm not that fragile either. You almost threw me into the truck," I said, frowning after being handled as if I were a sack of potatoes.

"Sorry. I was surprised at how light you seemed to be. I'll try to go easier on you from now on," Jake said with a guilty yet amused look.

2

After waiting for traffic to subside, Jake walked around and got in on the driver's side. "I have a note from my doctor that says I can't drive safely with a seat belt. It's too much pressure on the area of my spine that's swollen, but feel free to use yours. Did you notice all the stars out tonight? The nice thing about being here in the country without the light pollution of the cities is you can see all of the Milky Way on a clear night," Jake said.

"The night sky is beautiful here, Jake. I can't remember how long it's been since I took the time to notice. It seems I'm always preoccupied looking at my desk or computer screen instead of up at the sky. If you don't mind, I'll roll down the window to get some fresh country air for a change," I said.

Jake looked over to see Pam in profile with her head tilted back and long blonde tresses fluttering softly in the wind. She looked so relaxed and adorable it almost took his breath away.

I said, "Oh look, the moon is coming out from behind the clouds."

"Would you care to hear a little easy listening music? I have blended vocal CDs with Buble, Celine, Connick, Shania..."

"Thanks, I'd like that. Maybe it'll get my mind off the office, so I can unwind. I didn't realize I was so tired from the drive up here. Just give me a poke if I should nod off. This is just dreamy. What's playing now?" I asked without opening my eyes.

"'Canadian Sunset.' It reminds me of the ski weekends up north before I was shot. The next one will be "Wonderland by Night." It's a favorite instrumental of mine. Whoops! We're here already. Wait and let me get around to help you down from the truck. I'll try to be more careful with you this time," Jake said as he reached out and gently supported me under my shoulders while lowering me lightly to the ground. "See? You floated down like a butterfly."

I turned and saw the restored, brick-faced Victorian house with gingerbread trim was framed with hundreds of miniature white lights. "Oh, Jake, it's beautiful. Do they keep the tiny Christmas lights on year-round?"

"Yeah, I think it accentuates the architectural lines. Be careful not to catch your heels between the cobblestones," Jake cautioned.

"Aren't they unusual to use for a driveway?" I asked.

"They were trucked here special from Boston where a few of the streets are still paved with them. Originally, the cobblestones and the smaller bricks you'll see on the old fireplace inside were used as ballast for sailing ships when they returned to the colonies from England or the trip up here from Baltimore. Of course, the ships went back fully laden with raw materials."

"Boy, you really know all your facts and figures."

"I guess I'm an expert on trivia. I seem to just soak it up. Here let me get the door for you," Jake said. As if on cue when I stepped through the doorway, a little Italian man with a chef's hat and apron seemed to magically appear. "Hi,

Luigi. I've brought company. This is Pamela, up from New York City for the weekend."

"La mia casa è la tua casa! I'm a very pleased to meet you, Ms. Pamela. Please be seated over here at the table by the fire. I'll get my daughter Angelina to take your drink order."

On the way through to the dining room, I couldn't help but notice the brightly colored murals on all the walls. It felt as though I was being swept away to Italy. The colors were so rich that the trees, vineyards, and fishing ports seemed real enough that I could have walked into the scenes depicted on the walls and be there. The oil paintings of the angels and cherubs in the clouds on the coffered ceilings looked as though they could have been painted by Michelangelo. "This place is remote from all the major streets. How do they manage to stay in business?" I asked.

"Word of mouth. Oh, here's Angelina. Angelina, this is Pam."

"Pleased to meet you, Pam. Good evening, Jake. Would you care for wine this evening?"

Jake said, "Pam hasn't eaten, so something soft, light, and fruity. How about a bottle of Zibibbo wine?"

"Jake, I don't want to be carried out of here. What did you order?" I asked.

"Relax, Pam. It's a Muscat similar to California's mountain Rhine wines. Very mild and shouldn't upset your stomach before we get some food into you."

Puzzled, I said, "I didn't see a menu yet."

Jake replied with a knowing smile, "Luigi will take care of the selections. Trust me. You'll love it."

Just then, a man with a concertina entered the dining area singing Santa Lucia followed by a number of other songs in Italian before he switched to singing Volare in English. His accent sounded more French than Italian, but his voice was full and melodious. "Wow! It seems like we're on a gondola in a canal in Venice. You sure know how to impress a girl," I said, trying to figure out exactly who my dinner companion really was. He sure appeared to be every bit of a charming gentleman, but did he have ulterior motives?

Following an amazing meal and delightful conversation as we got better acquainted, time flew by much too fast. Jake bade farewell to Luigi and his daughter after leaving a generous tip for the singer who enraptured me with his serenades during dinner. After escorting me back to the truck, Jake was more cautious this time about assisting my entry to the cab.

"Jake, everything was absolutely delicious as promised. It's been a while since I've been out on a date. This is certainly different from the business luncheons and dinners I usually attend. Maybe it's because you resemble Michael so much that I feel we've known each other forever, but your personality is totally different from his. Thank you for insisting that I come tonight. I was hungrier than I thought, and I enjoyed the delightful company," I said.

"You're most welcome. I told you it wasn't very far from campus. Is that your car over there with the New York license plates?" Jake asked.

"Yes, that's it. It's not that late, but I'm totally bushed and need a good night's sleep. Thanks again for fabulous dinner and the fascinating conversation. I had a great time tonight."

"Pam, slow down a minute. I want to make sure you're safely checked into your motel room before I leave. There have been a couple of muggings in this area recently. Go ahead. I'll follow you," Jake said as he pulled out enough to block traffic, so I could get in front and lead the way to the Hampton Inn.

Although Jake had been a perfect gentleman all evening, I wondered what he could have been expecting when we got to my motel.

Upon our arrival, he got out of the truck and said, "If you unlatch your trunk, I'll get your bags while you check in."

When I returned from the office, I told him, "It's room 108 facing the back side. At least it'll be quiet because it's away from the highway noise, although I'm so tired I could probably sleep on an airport runway tonight."

Jake said with that beguiling grin of his, "I'll bring your bag to your room, but you're on your own if you want to take in an airport later," then followed me through the lobby.

As he helped me with the digital keycard and placed the luggage in the room, Jake asked, "Have you ever seen the

Berkshire hills in the spring?"

"No, I haven't."

"Great. You get a good night's sleep, and if you'd like me to, I can pick you up at nine in the morning. We can have breakfast on the way to the mountains."

"That sounds delightful, Jake. I'd love to. It'd certainly be different from life in the city. I'm sure it would do me a world of good to help me relax. I'll look forward to seeing you in the morning," I said as I leaned on the door frame, not quite sure if I really wanted the evening to end.

"Good night. I had a very nice time tonight too. Please make sure to use the chain and deadbolt," Jake said, pausing as if to say something before he changed his mind. Then he turned to walk down the hallway.

I closed and locked the door as Jake suggested, kicked off my heels, walked out of my skirt, and flopped on the bed. My head was spinning. I hadn't been out on a date in so long, I didn't know whether to shake Jake's hand or give him the big kiss I was tempted to. Instead I stood there like a doofus.

It had been ages since someone was that nice to me without ulterior motives, and I didn't know how to process that.

Putting up walls for self-protection really has left me isolated. I guess I'd reached a point where I only viewed males as the competition, especially the men I've worked with. Perhaps I was surprised that he appeared to be sincerely concerned about my welfare. I'd always been adept at deflecting direct assaults when men tried to hit on me, but this felt different. I didn't feel threatened in the least. I don't know how else to say it; he was just plain friendly.

This is silly. What could I have been thinking? Did I really want to get involved with someone? I hardly know him. For all I know, he could have been an ax murderer. Even if he was as wonderful as he seemed to be...if we had kissed... one thing could have led to another...

That's enough of this crazy talk. I almost had a vision of setting up housekeeping with Jake in a little vine-covered cottage. The next thing I knew, I would have had an urge to start knitting something, and I'm not even domesticated. Little wonder I'm confused. It must have been the effects of the wine on an empty stomach before I had a chance to eat.

It was just a night out over a fantastic dinner in a charming setting. Luigi and his daughter Angelina treated us like family and couldn't do enough for us. I was thrilled to get that much attention after being a veritable social hermit all these years. Still, if I was interested in finding someone, Jake seemed to have all the right qualifications, and he was certainly interesting and different from most men I'd met. I was just soooo tired and in need of a good night's sleep; I barely managed to phone for a wake-up call and slide under the covers.

3

I heard a knock, saw Jake's smiling face through the peephole viewer, and quickly opened the door. I had no idea why I was so glad to see him again, or why my heart was beating a little faster.

"Well, good morning, bright eyes," Jake said. "Mine usually look like two burnt holes in a blanket when I get up, but yours really sparkle."

"Good morning, Jake. Thank you for the compliment. I thought wearing shorts would allow me to hop up to the cab by myself, so you wouldn't throw your back out. You didn't say if formal attire would be required today. If it is, I can change or bring something else with me," I said.

"Nope, you're just fine as you are. Everything will be strictly casual. By the way, you look positively fantastic today," Jake said.

"Thank you again, Jake. If you keep this up, it'll go to my head."

"If you can wait a little while for breakfast, there's a little family restaurant called the Sugar House on a farm out on the Berkshire foothills portion of US Route 20 past the Blandford ski area. It'll be worth it, especially if you like

Belgian waffles with fresh strawberries and whipped cream or with their own maple syrup," Jake said.

I said, "That sounds wonderful. You sure are full of surprises."

He seemed very laid back for a professor, and it looked as though he was intent on spoiling me. I'd been accustomed to making decisions on my own, and here he was, giving my brain a serious chance to rest for a change.

"I'm sorry. I didn't mean to presume anything. I just figured I could serve as the designated regional representative and Indian guide for today since you haven't been in this area for years. Did I mention I am part Native American? My great grandmother was a Nipmuc. That hardly registers on the DNA scale, but it's in the bloodline. Your chariot awaits, madame," he said.

Jake extended his hand to help me into the truck, but as he opened the door, I grasped the handhold on the windshield frame and pulled myself up to the seat. He stood there with his mouth open and said, "If I didn't know better, I'd swear you'd been practicing that entry move all night. You really are graceful though. I'll have to award you with at least nine points for style, form, and execution."

"Just when I thought you were different from all the other guys. You weren't listening when I told you I work out at the gym."

Jake put in another CD of relaxing elevator music as we wound our way up the Berkshire foothills following the Westfield River on US Route 20. I leaned back in the seat and lost myself in the delightful music and the pleasant scenery of the hills, trees, and the river below.

"I think the place is around the next turn after the paper mill down in the valley. Yep, there it is." Jake said as he pulled off the highway.

"You didn't tell me it was a log cabin. How quaint," I said. "At least these hill folks have a sense of humor, Jake. Did you see the small picture frame underneath their Sugar House sign that reads, 'Home Sweet Home'?"

"No. I hadn't noticed it before. It is appropriate for a place that makes maple syrup though. Maybe they use the same gag writer that I do for my puns," Jake replied, grinning.

The outside of the log wall under the farmer's porch was covered with an antique washboard, galvanized tub, old fashion skis, handmade snowshoes, bear traps, and crosscut saws. Rough hewn picnic tables with red and white checkered tablecloths were set up underneath the overhang with wagon wheel chandeliers overhead.

"Would you like to eat inside or out here," Jake asked.

"Let's get some fresh air and sunshine out here if the bugs aren't too bad."

"No problem. The breezes at this elevation blow them away, so they don't get up this high. Here comes the waitress.

Have you decided what you'd like to order?"

"You talked me into the waffles with strawberries and whipped cream. I started salivating when you mentioned it earlier. Black coffee and a small orange juice would be great with that too," I said, removing my sunglasses to appreciate the view better. I reached across the table to take Jake's hand, since it seemed to be the natural thing to do. I was amazed that my hand all but disappeared when his encapsulated mine. His touch was warm but so gentle for someone his size.

Jake added, "I'll have the lumberjack special with scrambled eggs, home fries, whole wheat French toast, and sausage patties. I'd also like black coffee with that, please."

While waiting to be served, I had a chance to study Jake in the daytime with a clearer head. Once I got past his military bearing, upright posture, and broad shoulders, I encountered those intense blue eyes under bushy brows that made it difficult for me to look away. He had the commanding presence of an officer with a tempered version of an army haircut without a hair out of place. His square jaw shouted strength of character. The gentle crow's feet around the eyes toned down what might otherwise be construed as harsh features. When he reached out to clasp my hand wearing a broad smile that radiated warmth, his firm grip telegraphed I could count on him and trust his word. His baritone voice was comforting and spoke volumes. He was at once a man's man but extremely amicable at the same time. Little wonder, he had my full attention and curiosity. Exactly who was this guy, and why did he seem different than all the others?

I was still blowing on my coffee to cool it enough to sip, when the waitress returned with the order. "Boy, that was fast. Everything looks and smells so good. Oh! I just realized I left my cell phone in my car. It seems strange that I haven't used it since I arrived last night. To make a total break from the office, I didn't bring any of my other electronic equipment with me either. It's so quiet and peaceful up here, Jake. I can see the river winding its way down through the mountains. It's as though we've been swept away from my universe on a flying carpet to a magical forest. However do you find these places?"

Upon reflection, Jake said, "I like to go exploring every now and then in my truck. It gives me a chance to unwind and think. That's the Westfield River down there. It once powered the paper mills downstream. It empties into the Connecticut River and eventually Long Island Sound. You'd better eat before your waffles get cold, Pam. There'll be plenty of scenery to take in later."

After we finished a hearty breakfast and Jake settled up on the check, we climbed back into the truck to resume our westward journey up the Berkshire hills on US Route 20. "Wow. I had a bigger appetite today than I thought. You were right. Those waffles were absolutely scrumptious. What's next?" I asked.

"If I told you, it wouldn't be a surprise. We're almost there if I don't miss the turn."

"I noticed that you don't have a GPS. How do you manage without one?"

"Sometimes I have trouble with directions when the sun isn't out and there are too many turns in the road, but I don't want my life run by machines and little boxes. I have no delusions about curing my students' addiction to them, but I'd like them to learn how to think instead of pushing little buttons by rote. I leave my phone at home on nights and weekends. I just wish someone would make a decent compass that would work in an American made truck though. Ah, here's Willow Creek Road in Lennox. On the right is the Berkshire Scenic Railway Museum."

Jake pulled into the parking area and helped me out of the truck. This time I braced my hands on his broad shoulders, leaned against him, and lowered myself ever so slowly to the pavement as he held me with his hands around my waist. All the while, we looked deep into each other's eyes, and I was certain we had a connection going. I paused a moment before breaking eye contact, and reluctantly letting go.

After purchasing tickets in the museum for the full round trip, we went out to the train platform. In his best imitation of a railroad conductor's voice, Jake said, "We are about to board a hundred-year-old train with a steam powered locomotive on a twenty-mile journey to Stockbridge via Lee, Mass. We'll be cruising at a speedy fifteen miles per hour—all downhill on the map but will approach twenty-five miles per hour on the return trip. The entire journey will take approximately ninety minutes. The tracks follow alongside the Housatonic River, so we may see a few egrets and great blue herons."

Changing his tone, he said, "Here let me help you up the steps. We can board on the right side of the car, so the sun won't be in our eyes."

"Jake, this is so neat. I've never been on an old train before. It has the original green leather seats, and the windows actually open, even if they need to be propped up with small boards."

Once we were up to full speed, I said, "Everything looks so plush and green outside. What kind of quarry is that over there?"

"They call it a lime quarry, but it's actually an open pit mine. There is another location here in Lee, Mass. where they do extract marble that is a real quarry though."

Since the spring air was a little chilly with all the windows open, I naturally snuggled up to Jake for warmth, and he put his arm around my shoulder. I looked up and smiled, glad we could share the scenery and the train ride together. I told myself, *I could get used to this*, and settled back to enjoy the trip.

Along the way we saw a blue heron and several white egrets bobbing their heads in the water to catch fish, crawdads and frogs in the shallows of the river near the railroad track. It was not difficult to imagine that most of the untamed area abutting the river looked the same as when the Housatonic branch of the Mohican Indians still lived in the area.

As we passed through the town of Lee, everybody's backyard was exposed for all to see, as if the railway didn't exist if they ignored it. I was happy we had a chance to get to know each other better on this trip. I commented, "With all that smoke from the engine and the windows open, I'm glad we're not up in the first car." Then I whispered, "Jake, I noticed the man with the dark mustache and thick black hair ahead keeps turning around to look at us. It kind of gives me the creeps."

"You're probably imagining it. Maybe he recognizes me from campus. We do have a lot of foreign students," Jake said.

We disembarked at the Stockbridge station, and I used the facilities before walking through the museum there with Jake. Since the sun had shifted higher in the sky, we stayed on the right side when we boarded the last car to get a bit further away from the smoke from the locomotive and see the view to the east this time. My curiosity was piqued again when the same swarthy man with the middle eastern appearance followed us into the other car, but I was having such a great time being with Jake, I dismissed it from my mind.

Returning to the original station, we walked back to the truck and climbed in. On the way, I had glanced around to make sure the strange-looking man wasn't following us. Once we were underway, I said, "That was fascinating. It was so nice of you to take me all the way here to see the Berkshire Scenic Railroad."

"It was my pleasure, Pam, but we're not done yet. We're going to take Route 7 a little way north toward Pittsfield. It won't take long. Look at those hills up on the left."

"Oh my gosh! It's beautiful. The slopes are all covered with pink and white flowering shrubs."

"That's mountain laurel. The hills are part of October Mountain State Park that covers four towns. It's the largest state park in Massachusetts. Do you know where the bear went?"

"What bear?"

"Remember the song 'The Bear Went over the Mountain'? Well here we go up to the top," Jake said, turning off the highway to a side street.

After a few miles, I said, "Jake, are you sure this road goes all the way through? We just ran out of pavement, and it's starting to rain hard."

"I went across the mountain on this road last year and didn't have any problem. We can turn around if you want though. Uh-oh, it's getting muddy. I thought it would have dried up this late in the season. I'll try to turn around as soon as the road gets a little wider. Nope, too late. The wheels are just spinning. It feels like we're stuck," Jake said as he tried to rock the truck back and forth to get some traction.

"Jake, what do you mean we're stuck? Don't you have four-wheel drive?"

"I never needed it before. I've been driving on back dirt roads for five years with this truck and never had a problem," Jake said. "It must have been all mud at the bottom of the huge puddle I was trying to get through. We're bottomed out and can't move. I'm sorry, Pam. All those heavy rains we had this spring must have saturated the ground."

"Oh great. The one time I really need my cell phone, and it's in my car. What are we going to do? I didn't bring any warm clothes with me. How cold does it get up on October Mountain at night?" I asked.

Jake reached behind the seat and pulled out a windbreaker jacket to put over my shoulders. "It won't get to freezing. Maybe it'll drop down to the low 40s. We'll just have to wait for someone to come along. The park rangers patrol these roads. I'm sure they'll come by before dark. We can't try to hike the five miles or so down to the highway until this downpour lets up.

I've got a couple of sleeping bags we can zip together. There's also a queen-sized air mattress under the cap to keep us above the steel truck bed, so we can stay warm. I threw a few sandwiches and drinks in the cooler back there in case we wanted to have a picnic somewhere today. Are you hungry?" Jake asked.

"Not yet. It's nice and warm here in the truck with the engine running, but we could make some heat of our own, so we don't run out of gas. Did I just say that out loud? I don't know what came over me. It does seem as though we've known each other forever, and we can talk about anything. I just feel safe as long as you're here with me, Jake... Jake, say something."

"I don't know where this is going. I guess I feel the same way you do. It should be way too soon to tell, but it seems as though we're meant to be together. It feels so right. Then again, you work in the city, and I'm up here. That's a long distance to commute. First things first, when the rain lets up a little we can get in back and make sure everything's situated before it gets too dark. I used the air mattress a few weeks back to stay overnight when I was trying to get early morning photographs of eagles and red-tailed hawks at the Quabbin Reservoir, but it might need to be blown up again." I snuggled up to Jake, and we shared our very first kiss. It was wonderful and seemed to last forever. The tingles it sent up my spine were electric, and I was encompassed in a warmth that I'd never experienced before with anyone else. It felt so comfortable to be alone with him out in the elements on top of a mountain that the rest of the world disappeared for me. We were the only two people left on earth that existed. It was destiny for this to be our time and place.

Turning over on the bench seat, I put my head in his lap while he just looked down at me with those piercing blue eyes that seemed to look right through me and see my soul. He smiled, and I felt like I could have melted down into a puddle myself.

Then he said, "Hey, Pam, the rain seems to be slowing down a little. Grab whatever you need, and let's get in the back in case it starts coming down in buckets again. You can zip the sleeping bags together while I pump the air mattress up again."

We slogged through the mud to get to the back. Jake gave me an assist to get up on the tailgate. Once we were settled inside and removed our wet, muddy shoes and socks, we unrolled the two sleeping bags and zipped them together before we slid in. The mattress seemed to be firm enough without pumping it up.

My bare legs felt cold until we were sitting in the sleeping bags. With Jake's jacket on and his arm around me, I soon felt toasty as I warmed my feet against Jake's legs.

Then we decided we were hungry after all and Jake asked, "Would you like to try some Lambrusco? I understand it's guaranteed to warm the cockles of your heart. I made the roast beef sandwiches with lettuce, tomato, and mayo. There's fried chicken and potato salad in here too."

I said, "You thought of everything. Are you sure you didn't plan all of this? Yes, I'll have wine and a sandwich. Don't tell me you even thought of napkins too? You know between the wine, sleeping bags, and you, I'm sure I'll be warm enough tonight."

Jake had two sandwiches to my one, but I was full, and it was so cozy in the sleeping bags zipped together like that. He was so yummy; I just wanted to take a bite out of him too.

"Did you have enough to eat? You can't keep nibbling on my ear and fogging up all the windows. If somebody comes to help us out, we won't be able to see them," Jake said.

"You implied that could be a bad thing. What would you say if I told you that I don't care if we make it back in time for the reunion tomorrow night?" I said.

Jake didn't know quite how to respond. Pam was coming on to him, and this had never happened to him before by someone that aggressive. In reality, he thought this was absolutely fantastic. How could he have lucked out to find a bright, intelligent woman who was absolutely drop dead gorgeous be that interested in him? While everything seemed to be going great, he wondered if he shouldn't tell her to slow down. Instead he said, "Well we could either stay here until the food runs out, or I could set up some traps to catch small game. How do you feel about hasenpfeffer?" "What's that?" I asked.

"Rabbit stew, but we 'll need to save some of the wine to make the recipe work. I can probably find enough fiddler ferns at this time of year for the stew and a salad. Darn it."

"Now what?" I asked, wondering what could possibly spoil all of this when everything seemed to be going so perfectly.

"I see a jeep approaching with flashing lights," he said. "It must be the park rangers. Do you suppose we could ask them to come back and rescue us tomorrow?"

Jake reluctantly turned away from me and slid out of the sleeping bags just as things were getting interesting. After he managed to slip back into his muddy shoes, he jumped down from the tailgate and stepped over the deep rut made by the truck. He sloshed over to the ranger in the army surplus jeep and said, "Hi, we were trying to get over the mountain and didn't realize the road was impassable."

Following a quick discussion with the ranger, Jake came back to his truck. "Pam, he said he has a cable and a winch. If you sit in the driver's seat and keep the wheel straight, I'll attach the hook to the frame and throw some of that brush under the front wheels. Then I can push from the back."

I put my muddy running shoes back on and slogged my way to the cab when Jake said, "Start it up and just give it a little gas when he's ready...okay, now...not too much... That's great...almost there...just a little further... You got it! I'll take off the hook. Thank you so much, sir."

I slid over to the passenger side and looked into the glove compartment to see if Jake had any Kleenex, but I was surprised to find a rather large revolver with a box of shells. When Jake got back into the truck, splattered with mud, I said, "I was looking for a tissue and opened your glove box. Why do you need to take a gun with you?"

"I have a permit in case I encounter bears or rabid animals when I'm out taking pictures of wildlife. There are tissues behind your seat." As we started to drive down the other side of October Mountain, Jake added, "The ranger said taking the road ahead would be better than trying to go back the way we came up. It will take about an hour to get back to Irving. Do you want to do that or see if we can find a motel for the night?"

"I was just getting warmed up before we were so rudely interrupted by the ranger. Let's find a motel with a king sized bed that I can chase you around on," I said, surprising myself, but glad I said it to let Jake know how I felt.

"This is weird. I've never been out with a fully liberated woman before. I'm not complaining you understand, but it does take some getting used to. For the record, I'm definitely attracted to you as well."

I replied, "I don't understand it either. It makes no sense, and it's not like me at all, but let's go with it and see where it leads."

Jake said, "There's a Best Western Motel ahead with a vacancy sign lit up. I'll see what they can do for us."

He returned from the office and told me, "The only thing they have available is one room with a single queen-sized bed, so you won't have to chase me as far. I didn't tell him we don't have any luggage. I'll need to pop into the shower to try to get this mud off me and wash my clothes, so they'll be dry by morning."

"Okay, but I get to scrub you down in the shower. Then you can return the favor," I said.

Jake grinned and said, "Only if you make sure you pay careful attention to the important parts."

Jake had been covered with mud on the mountain when the wheels were spinning, so he went into the shower fully clothed. I stripped down and hurried to join him after collecting the extra bars of soap under the sink. I put my arms around him, looked up, and said, "Hey, big guy, move over and make room for me. I've been waiting to get you cornered like this."

Jake backed up, pulled me closer, and said, "Wow! On a scale of one to ten, you have to be at least an eleven. You didn't need to corner me; I'm not going anywhere."

"Calm down and keep your pants on until we clean the mud off your clothes," I said. "Now let's see, where were we? I believe we were in the back of your truck when that ranger came along. Then what? Oh, that was it. I don't know all the reasons, but I was becoming strangely attracted to you. I was just about to get to the bottom of it in the sleeping bag when we had to stop. Tell you what we're going to do. You are going to stay perfectly still and not say anything while I scrub the mud off and try to figure that out. Once we get that out of the way, we can wash each other."

"Okay, that takes care of washing the shirt and pants. I'm having a little trouble getting your zipper past an obstacle that arose. Well, what do we have here? It appears to be a snake peeking out, and he only has one eye. I'll try to coax him past those restraints. Look at that, the little guy is reaching out. I bet he wants to shake hands. He seems to like it, so maybe I'll humor him for a while. Uh-oh, the snake spit at me. That's it. The punishment for being naughty is a time-out in the penalty box. Get him over here.

He does feel nice and warm. Maybe we can let him move around for a while. Oh, Jake, maybe this was one of the missing reasons. Kiss me."

"Pam, you sure are good at doing laundry. I never knew I needed help. I don't know why I've never tried washing my clothes like this before."

"I never have either, Jake. It definitely is much more fun this way, and there's only one thing to plug in to make it work. You know they say most accidents happen in the bathtub. Hold me close while we wash each other, so we don't slip and fall."

"Don't worry I've got your back." Jake said. "As soon as I finish that side, you can turn around, and I'll do your front."

"Is that when I get to do the important part?" I asked.

"As long as he ends up squeaky clean and you don't wear him out," Jake said.

"If he soils himself again, we'll just have to keep washing him off. Tell him no more spitting though, or there'll be additional consequences. I'll put extra soap on him, so he can help with the cleaning," I said.

When the clothes were washed and rinsed, we lingered so long in the shower discovering each other, we used up two motel-sized bars of soap. Jake's muscles were certainly well concealed when he had clothes on, especially the one he thought was important; but in the end, they were well scrubbed as were my breasts and all my other parts. They had never been cleaner.

"Pam, this is the best shower I've ever taken. Thank you for sharing," Jake said.

We tried to hold a kiss as we toweled each other off, but something cropped up again. We staggered to the bed while we were still soaking wet, locked in an embrace.

Some things just couldn't wait and required immediate attention. We spent our first night together like a pair of overanxious newlyweds in an endurance contest. I'm sure we would have won regardless of the competition.

Jake's staying power was absolutely amazing. Forget about climbing the walls, I thought I'd have to be scraped off the ceiling. Between the third and fourth time, Jake hopped off the bed to hang his clothes up, so they'd be dry by morning.

When I decided the sunlight filtering in the cracks next to the curtain was bright enough to indicate it was time to get up, I asked, "Did you manage to get any sleep at all, Jake?"

"Even being totally exhausted, it was wonderful holding you in my arms for the rest of the night, but I must have drifted off and slept for a couple of hours anyway. I couldn't believe your stamina. I thought you said you were out of practice. It sure didn't look that way to me."

"I was, but it's just like riding a bicycle—or in your case—a pogo stick. Maybe it was because I was starved for attention."

"Do you still want to go to the reunion tonight?"

"I haven't really decided. We could stay here and fool around instead," I said.

"I didn't think you were fooling around, Pam. You looked pretty serious to me.

You should go to your reunion though. You haven't seen these people in twenty years. It'd be nice to catch up with them to see how they turned out and what they're doing now. It could provide some perspective on your priorities in life. Besides, they might be good contacts for your business."

“I hadn’t thought about that. Maybe you’re right. What about us?”

Jake said, “What about us? How can you think there’s an *us*? Just because we’ve had a wonderful thirty-six hours together? Dinner was delightful. Travel was terrific. Our shower was stupendous. The motel was magnificent. What does that add up to other than possibly a great beginning of something that could become positively scintillating?

We should slow down a little and try to figure out where we’re at and where can we go from here. That doesn’t mean we can’t continue to have fun while we do that.”

“So, what you’re saying is that we have found nothing in common so far other than fascinating conversation, wonderful companionship, mutual interests, and super sex. Sounds like a very good start to me. Let’s go have a big breakfast. I worked up another monstrous appetite,” I said.

Jake said, “I want to be sure we’re both on the same page. Neither one of us has had a sustained, long-term relationship, certainly not recently. This could be a case of infatuation, pent-up emotions, or overactive hormones. Unless we buy a couple of boats to meet on weekends where the Connecticut River joins Long Island Sound in New Haven, you’re in New York City, and I’m in Massachusetts. After our brief time together, all I can say at this point is that you’re a beautiful, lovely woman, and I’m very much in like with you.”

“When you put it that way, I’m very much in like with you too. Now come back to bed, so I can show you how much all over again. We can always have breakfast some other time,” I said.

4

We behaved like we hadn't been at it all through the night until we finally fell apart, gasping for breath, soaking wet with perspiration, tangled in the sheets, and totally exhausted, but sated at last. Once we managed to roll off the mattress, we met at the end of the bed, gently embraced, and managed to hold a kiss while slowly wandering to the shower as if tied together by an invisible cord. Even with the temperature of the shower unadjusted, we were oblivious to the fact that the water was freezing cold as we took turns caressing each other with the single bar of soap between us. Still not a word was spoken while we tenderly toweled each other off and continued to stare as though seeing our partner for the very first time.

As if what happened on our first night together was a common occurrence, while we were getting dressed, I asked, "Since most of my classmates will bring a spouse or date to the DUI reunion, would you like to take me?"

"Of course, I'd be happy to," Jake said. "Can you give me a breakdown of what's expected and timelines? Do I just wear grown-up pants, or is this a suit and tie deal?"

I said, "I think it will be on the dressy side of casual. No tie or jacket required. Cocktails and get reacquainted reception at five, dinner at six, and dancing after seven. I never asked, you do know how to dance, don't you?"

Jake said, "Knowing how and doing are two different things entirely. On a good night, I can hold my own. If my back is giving me grief, I'm limited to multiple slow dances without excessive twisting and turning. As long as you don't let any of those fast women cut in. Then you'll be stuck with me for the duration. "If I'm having any problems, I can always stand in the middle of the floor, and you could dance around me. I'll give you a wink as you pass by. Just remember that a wink is as good as a nod."

I said, "I don't know about this. It could end up more complicated than I thought it would be. If you put a lampshade on your head, I'll pretend I don't know you and say you've been stalking me.

"Unbelievable! I just realized; I don't know your last name. I could just introduce you as Jake the date. Is it Porter like your cousin Michael?"

"Nope, it's Wells. Our mothers were sisters. Oddly enough, you never told me your last name either. Since we already did our one-night stand, I probably should know what it is."

"It's Mullen. Pam Mullen."

"Great. Pleased to meet you, Ms. Mullen, Pam Mullen," Jake said. "Now I don't have to wait to read your nametag tonight to find out. How are they going to fit 'Ms. Pamela Mullen, vice president of finance at Grady Trading Company' all on the same label with your graduation picture? I like it though. It doth roll trippingly off the tongue, but maybe it could be shortened to Pamela Mullen, VP of F. We won't have to say what the initials stand for. I could give them a hint and tell them the VP stands for very pretty, but they can see that for themselves."

"Why, Professor Wells, I'm surprised you finally noticed. I was beginning to feel ignored."

"You know I would never do that to you. Since you look as tired as I feel, I'll help you into the truck and then go check out," Jake said.

We returned to the truck, and as we got on the highway again, Jake said, "Since we seem to be joined at the hip this weekend, it might be simpler to check you out of the Hampton Inn and you could stay at my place if you want. That way we could both get ready at my house later this afternoon."

"It sounds like a good idea."

"Would you like to do lunch on the return trip? How do you feel about a Chinese buffet at the Golden Peacock?" Jake asked.

"That would be okay with me. I can check out and pick up my car after we eat. Then I'll follow you home."

We pulled into the parking lot of the Golden Peacock Restaurant where the outside looked like a Chinese pagoda with several colors of koi fish swimming in the little moat next to the front door. "This restaurant looks kind of neat," I said.

Jake held the door open for me, and I said, "I love the interior decorations with all the bright colors, plants, and lanterns. It's amazing that all those fish in the aquariums can coexist without the smaller ones getting eaten. "I need to find the ladies' room. Please order hot tea for me if the server comes for our order before I get back. From the looks of all the selections over at the buffet, I'll go with that."

I returned from the rest room and said, "Ta da! Here I am. All fixed up. I didn't get a chance to put on makeup this morning."

Jake said, "I sure didn't notice Pam, but you looked lovely even when you were naked."

"Jake! Is that all you ever think about?" I asked, trying to appear to be shocked, but pleased he thought so.

"I meant naked as in 'when you didn't have any makeup on.' You looked fantastic without it," Jake clarified. "You've been the aggressor so far. You do look beautiful when you are naked too, but I didn't want to bring it up in a public place. There's no telling what could happen or what you're capable of. We might get thrown out of here if we were to start anything on the carpet."

"I don't know what's come over me. I've never been this way before, ever. It must be because of you. This isn't me. It's not who I am, or who I thought I was," I said, confused.

"Well whoever you are pretending to be, you are doing one heck of a job, and I appreciate it. I hope this isn't typical of your behavior in all those business meetings though," Jake said, smiling.

"Can we change the subject? All this talk is making me excited all over again. It looks like they have a big selection of food at the buffet tables. Shall we go fill our plates?" I said as I stood up. "I'm hungry after missing breakfast."

"That's your own fault, lady. The motel offered a free continental breakfast. It was you that wanted the extra time messing around in the sack," Jake said on the way to the buffet. "By the way, I enjoyed it too. Thank you very much."

Jake had already returned to the table while I was still having trouble trying to decide what to select. As I sat down, I said, "I hope I didn't take too much. Everything looked so good I couldn't fit it all on my plate. I should have done a better job of pacing myself."

Jake must have been astonished at the amount of food piled on my plate when he commented, "Wow! Don't they feed you down in the city? Don't forget, I'm in no shape to drag you all over the dance floor. It's little wonder you have to do all those exercises. If you don't kill me dancing, maybe we can burn off a few of those calories tonight when we get back after the reunion," he said, wiggling his eyebrows and grinning.

Trying not to talk with a full mouth, I said, "I love duck, but this is nothing short of phenomenal, especially for a buffet. It melts in your mouth and isn't the least bit greasy. You sure know how to pick your restaurants."

"Was the duck Peking at you over the edge of the chafing dish or just calling your name?" Jake asked.

I said, "The next thing I know is that you'll want to keep it as a pet and give it a name. Everything I've tried so far has been delicious. I might have to dig all the way down to my plate, so I don't miss anything. Of course, I'm not sure what I'm eating with each forkful, but it all tastes great."

"At least you didn't try to show me up by using the chopsticks. I never could figure out how to use them to get the food all the way up to my mouth," Jake said. "If you like this, I'll have to take you to a Thai restaurant. Their food tends to be a little lighter and less greasy if you stay away from the heavier peanut sauces."

"For obvious reasons, my business luncheons and dinners don't include Asian restaurants. I'd almost forgotten how good they can be. Do you realize that we keep talking like this will go on forever between us? We just met. How is that possible that we can know each other so well, so fast?" I asked.

"It sure beats me. Was it timing? I've never made this kind of connection with anyone like this before. Especially this soon. It do boggle the mind, don't it?" Jake said. "I don 't know about you, but I am absolutely stuffed. Unless you want dessert, let's read our fortune cookie tags, pay the bill, and get on the road again. What does yours say?"

"'You are always welcome in any gathering.' That must mean everything will go well at the reunion tonight."

"Mine says, 'Stop searching forever. Happiness is just next to you.' They certainly have us pegged," Jake added.

5

As Jake unlocked the passenger door, I was in the seat before he knew it. Jake exclaimed, "Wow! You're becoming a pro at hopping up into the cab unassisted."

When we got back on the road again, I asked, "Does this armrest fold up out of the way?"

"Only if you transfer the stuff that's in the center arm compartment first to one of the plastic bags behind the seat. Why do you ask?" he inquired.

"Why indeed? Because I want to snuggle up to you while you drive, you big silly. That's why," I said.

"All right, but no nibbling or tickling," Jake ruled. "You realize that with the armrest in the full, upright position you'll have unimpeded access to the driver. Before seat belts were mandatory, we had a couple of names for that when I was a teenager. Going around a curve fast, a COD was a come-over-darling, and a SOB was called a slide-over-baby."

"I never heard of those before. We must have grown up in different time zones. Mmmm. This is much better," I said, cuddling up behind his right shoulder. "I could become very accustomed to this."

"Don't get too rambunctious. Traffic is picking up, and we don't have that far to go," Jake said.

As we approach my motel, Jake said, "I'll park next to your car and round up your luggage while you check out. Then you can follow me home."

We went to the room, and once I repacked my bags, Jake took them back to the truck. I got the receipt from the room that was billed to my credit card and followed him home in my car. We turned off the main road to a long dirt driveway, and Jake pulled up next to a house that couldn't be seen from the road.

When we got out, I said, "This is beautiful, perfectly charming. It's such an adorable cottage. You didn't tell me you lived on a lake. It's so peaceful and quiet."

He explained, "That's because it's called Brook's Pond, and due to its small size, the local regulations limit boat motors to 15 horsepower, which minimizes the noise levels. Just when we're convinced we know everything about each other, something else pops up. Maybe we should start writing things down.

I'll bring your bags into the guest room. The bureau and closet are empty, so there'll be plenty of room for your things. You'll have to excuse the mess in the kitchen. I didn't make time to clean up yesterday after I filled the picnic cooler, just in case."

"I love your home. Everything is so cozy with all the furnishings and the fireplace flanked by the bookcases. I was surprised to see the antique love seat though," I said because it didn't match the rest of the decor.

"It came from my grandmother's house after she passed away. It meant so much to her I didn't have the heart to part with it," Jake said.

"I'm just starting to realize I'm very tired after that big meal. Since you have a king size bed, do you think we have time for a little nap before we get ready?"

"I can't believe I'm saying this, but only if you calm down. No more shenanigans this afternoon. Otherwise we'll never get to your reunion. If you remember correctly, that's why you came back to DUI," Jake said with a stern expression.

"You are starting to sound like my father, but okay. I promise to behave. As long as we can curl up together. Can you please set the alarm for three? I'll need at least that much time to get ready for tonight," I said.

Being exhausted from lack of sleep, we conked out as soon as our heads hit the pillows, entwined in each other's arms. Much too soon, the alarm went off, and we wondered if we really wanted to separate long enough to get ready for the evening before us. Being that close to Jake was becoming both delicious and habit forming.

Having freshened up my lipstick and makeup, I slipped into my indispensable little black dress I usually wore to business dinners. Since Jake was nearby, I held up my hair and turned my back, so he could zip me up. Based on the night we had just shared together; it might not have been the wisest thing to do. No sooner was I zipped then Jake was kissing the nape of my neck, and I almost wilted.

Jake apologized once he recognized I was enjoying it as much as he was. He threw his hands in the air and said, "Okay, okay, I'll let you finish getting dressed, but you look so utterly ravishing in that outfit and waaay too hard to resist."

Just then the telephone on the end table in the bedroom rang. Jake glanced at the caller ID then hurried to pick it up on the kitchen wall phone. I could barely hear Jake's voice modulate somewhere between a mumble and a whisper. I inferred that a sensitive matter was being discussed. Not wanting to pry, I combed out my hair and was putting on my pearls as he returned to the bedroom to grab his watch and keys. For just an instant, I wondered what he could possibly have to be secretive about, but he seemed nice enough otherwise.

I said, “I’m all set,” as I grabbed my clutch purse from the bureau. Walking out to the truck, it was beginning to feel natural to have Jake hoist me up to the seat but kissing him on the nose in the process meant I had to wipe off the lipstick after.

6

As we approached campus, Jake turned to me and asked, "Did I mention that you look positively radiant tonight?"

I said, "Yes, you did while I was still combing out my hair. Thank you again. It's probably because you do such a fantastic job of turning me on."

"I've got a campus parking permit for any lot, but I can drop you off by the door if you'd prefer," Jake said.

"It's such a lovely evening; we can walk from the truck. It's not that far."

At the table set up in front of the ballroom entrance, I said, "Hi. I'm Pam Mullen, and this is my date Jake Wells. We called ahead to say there would be one more coming. I think we owe you another $50 for the extra dinner."

Once inside, I told Jake, "I have my nametag, but you're on your own if you wander off. Just remember to save the last dance for me."

As I turned, the first person I saw took a minute for me to recognize. She had much longer hair than the pixie cut she used to wear when she was younger. "Jenni! Is that you? Other than your hair style, you haven't changed a bit," I said.

“Pam, we’ve missed our ringleader at the previous reunions. And of course, I’d know Michael anywhere,” she said, giving me a big hug.

“Jenni, this is Jake Wells who happens to bear a striking resemblance to his cousin Michael Porter. Don’t ask, it’s a very long story, and you wouldn’t believe it if I told you anyway.

“Jake, this is Jenni Crowfoot of the Blackfoot Tribe in Alberta, Canada. She was one of my dearest friends in college and a sorority sister.”

“Jenni, I’m pleased to meet you,” Jake said shaking her hand. “My Nipmuc forebears were driven out of southern New England to Nova Scotia for a while, but some of them managed to find their way back down. Maybe our Indian ancestors were related somehow.”

“Pam, I don’t know where or how you found Jake, but I think you ought to keep him anyway. Tell me what have you been doing with yourself for the last twenty years?” Jenni asked.

I said, “I’ve been in finance for a brokerage firm on Wall Street. It’s kept me pretty busy. How about you?”

Jenni said, “I went back to teach high school at the Alberta Indian Reservation in Canada. It doesn’t pay much, but it is extremely rewarding. I have two kids of my own who are now in college. Fortunately, they are both on partial academic scholarships, so that helps a lot.

My husband works in the oil fields. He rotates four weeks straight followed by a week off. The separation is terrible, but it’s so nice when he finally can come home for a week at a time. With that schedule, the fact that we only have two children is amazing unto itself. The oil drilling company is one of the few places in the area that pays well.

“Listen to me go on and on. I see Patty over there, and I did want to talk with her too. Make sure you find me again later, so we can finish catching up. It was nice to meet you, Jake, even if we didn't give you a chance to get a word in edgewise."

"After twenty years, I'm sure you and Pam still have a lot to catch up on. It was a pleasure to meet you as well," Jake replied.

"Boy, your friend Jenni is some talker," Jake said, once Jenni caught up with Patty. "I was beginning to wonder if she would take a breath."

"It looks like they're starting to file into the dining area Jake. Watch for my name place label or the Sigma Kappa sorority table," I said.

As he looked around the room, Jake said, "Okay. It looks like the sorority, and fraternity tables are on the left. The only one I see with two Greek letters is in the corner."

"There's only one couple there so far," I said. "Come on over, and I'll introduce you. Hi, Barbara. This is Jake, my escort for the evening."

Barbara smiled and said, "Hi, Pam. I'm so glad you could make it to this reunion. We've missed you. This is my husband, Jon. Did you know Pam was the unofficial organizer for almost every Sigma Kappa event? She was very shy but totally efficient."

Jake said as he shook hands, "How do you do? I can believe Pam was well organized but shy? I was under the impression that she was exceptionally aggressive. Then again, we 've only recently met."

"Pam, you'll have to tell me all about how that happened while Jon and Jake talk about sports or some other guy stuff," Barbara said with a wave of her hand while she turned her back on her husband and Jake.

I said, "Barbara, you look wonderful. There's really not much to tell. We met in the Kenwood Diner Thursday night, and it started over coffee..."

When everyone else started to file in and take a seat, I ended up sitting next to Jenni with Barbara sitting across the table during the meal. Jon was on the opposite side of Jake, so they could talk about something other than what sorority life was like twenty years ago. After dinner was served, Jake finally got a word in when Jenni and Barbara were talking about another topic.

Jake said, "Pam, the New England clam chowder and Boston baked scrod were great even by Cape Cod standards. I'll bet you'd have trouble finding anything close to that in New York. I really missed good seafood when I lived in Minnesota. It was tough to get a decent meal in a restaurant out there."

"It's getting to be difficult to find a really good restaurant in New York as well." I said.

Jake said, "In the Midwest they even ship all their choice and prime beef to the east coast, so the better places in New York must have decent beef available. The stockyards in St. Paul passed Chicago in volume years ago because that's where the livestock belt meets the grain belt of the Great Plains.

Since they're starting to clear the dinner dishes, did you want to dance while we're waiting for dessert?"

"Good timing, Jake. They're playing a waltz. We can start off slow and see how well that works," I said.

When we got out on the dance floor, I put my head on Jake's shoulder, and he asked, "What did Barbara say earlier about you being painfully shy? That's not the girl of my dreams I met this weekend. Would you care to run that horse by me again?"

I looked up and said, "That was in another lifetime. I've been running with the big dogs of the business world in Gotham City since then. I can't be backed down or threatened by anyone and still survive. That doesn't mean I'm not socially shy, or at least I thought I was when I drove up here. Then I met you and realized what I'd been missing. Perhaps it is finally time for me to get a life of my own. After all, I've earned it."

Jake said, "Nobody's arguing with you on that score. But with you rubbing up against me like this, I might be embarrassed when I try to sit down. Do you think you could back off a tad and put a little space between us?"

"I'm so sorry. It just felt so nice to be this close to you I didn't even realize I was getting a rise out of you. By the way, you dance just fine. I don't even have to lead. I'm glad I wore the stiletto heels, so I can reach high enough to kiss you on the neck," I said as I blotted my lipstick just above his collar.

It was kind of like marking my territory.

7

The reunion flew by all too fast. Dancing all the slower songs with Jake was absolutely wonderful, but in between I didn't seem to have enough time to catch up with as many old friends as I wanted to. It was too bad that I didn't attend the other reunions to keep track of what was going on in everyone else's life. Still it was great to see my classmates after all these years. Apparently, most were impressed, but not surprised by my success.

On our way back to Jake's house, I said, "Thank you so much for taking me to the reunion tonight. I dreaded the thought of going by myself when most of the attendees would have a spouse or significant other along. It was so nice to see them again, especially Jenni. They may be strapped for cash, but it sounds like they have a very rewarding life. I've really missed not seeing her all these years."

"I'm glad that you had a good time, Pam. Since it is a little on the hot and humid side tonight, what would you say to a little swim to cool off before we turn in?" Jake asked.

"That sounds nice, but I didn't bring a bathing suit."

"And because you have always been so quiet, shy, and retiring, you never dared to try skinny dipping in the moonlight?" Jake said.

"How could you even suggest that? Somebody would see us," I said, surprised that Jake would think I'd even consider it.

"My dock is in a secluded little cove, enclosed by the trees. It's all but invisible to everyone else on the pond. I have a couple of sit-on-top kayaks we can lie on and gaze up at the stars. Besides, I'm supposed to be doing my aqua therapy exercises anyway. You could help." Jake said with a big smile while doing that thing he does with his eyebrows.

"Won't you take a chance of hurting your back that way?" I asked.

"Actually, I can move a lot easier with the buoyancy of the water. Then you won't have to do all the work for a change," Jake said.

"Hey, I'm not complaining. I just can't understand how I could have missed all those years without having sex. Maybe it was because I never found the right partner until now," I said, trying to sound seductive while reaching over to run my fingers through his hair.

As he turned down his long driveway, Jake responded, "It certainly is a totally different experience with you. I was just thinking about a line from an old movie, maybe it was Jerry Maguire. He said, 'You complete me.' That definitely seems to be the case here. It's hard to fathom how we can possibly be this good together."

Jake pulled up to the house and helped me down from the truck. We walked hand in hand to the house, and as we entered the front door, he said, "When we go out to the dock, I'll turn off the porch lights. May I get you something to drink while we change out of these party clothes? I'll find you a robe and get a couple of beach towels."

I said, "A beer would be great about now. Do you have anything lite?"

"Sorry. Only have real beers that begin with an M. I like Millers, Molson, Michelob, and Moosehead. I wasn't expecting company this weekend. How would a Miller High Life in a frosted mug be?" Jake asked.

"That sounds great. My mouth is a little dry. Maybe I'm a little nervous because I've never tried skinny dipping or making love in the water before," I said, wondering if I was really up for either.

Jake returned with a pair of frosted mugs of beer and an extra robe for me that he found in the closet. We stepped out the door as the clouds moved in front of the moon. There was still enough moonlight to see where we were walking, but the dew on the grass felt strange on my bare feet.

"Are you sure nobody can see us?" I asked as I removed the robe and placed it on the dock, so it would be available, just in case.

"Look around. Can you see or hear anybody else from here?" Jake said.

I said, "What I hear is almost a deafening cacophony of birds, frogs, and crickets. I think I just heard a splash from a fish jumping too. The moon is so bright again it's almost like daylight. I'd forgotten how nice it is being outside in the country at night."

Jake said, "Let me set the mugs down on the dock and spread out the towels on the kayaks. I'll help you get balanced on top of one of the boats. Then I'll hand you the beers to hold while I get on the other kayak.

Did I mention that you look absolutely gorgeous when you're naked in the moonlight? Even Aphrodite would pale by comparison to the intoxicating vision of you, the fairest of maidens. The twinkling in thine eyes tonight doth put the very stars to shame for their lackluster appearance. Truth be told, the moment seems so magical; I half expect you to sprinkle me with fairy dust any minute now lest I awake from this wondrous dream."

I was surprised to hear all this coming from Jake, and I said, "Somehow I never thought an engineer could wax poetic, but please don't stop. I love it. Jake, be careful getting on. You'll tip us both over."

"And the penalty for that would be what? We'd both get wet when we fall in?" he said.

"No, you'll spill my beer, and I wouldn't be as uninhibited as I want when I attack you in the moonlight," I replied, amazing myself with how bold I'd become with Jake.

"In that case, I have another six pack of beer in the fridge. Shall I go get more to make sure you're appropriately lubricated?" Jake asked with his smile gleaming in the moonlight like a Cheshire cat.

"Don't you dare," I said. "I want to be fully conscious of everything that transpires. I don't want to miss out on any part of our encounters. They're much too delightful. I know it's much too soon to know for sure, but I think I'm beginning to zip right past being in like with you."

We enjoyed an enchanted evening in the water filled with the wonder of our newly discovered love. With little sleep the night before, we reluctantly retired to the king sized bed but only used a small part of it when we snuggled closely together in what now seemed to be the only natural and perfect thing to do.

8

Sleeping until almost noon, we brunched on the sun-splashed porch overlooking the pond while we enjoyed the chirping of birds, chatter of chipmunks, flutter of butterflies, and hummingbirds searching for their next cluster of flowers.

I had a book in my lap that I couldn't concentrate on with my head still spinning because I was thinking about the unbelievable weekend we had enjoyed together. I looked up at Jake and said, "Jake, skinny dipping and making love with you in the water were wonderful last night. I suddenly feel as though I've been leading a very sheltered existence and missing out on too many of the truly amazing things life has to offer. I hate to think about having to leave you to drive back to New York City today for that meeting first thing in the morning. Where can we get together next weekend?"

"I'm afraid we can't possibly do that, Pam. I already have plans," Jake said, frowning.

Suddenly, I felt as though I had slammed into a brick wall at full speed. "What do you mean? Is there someone else?" I asked, stunned.

"No, there isn't anybody else. I have long standing plans that can't be changed," Jake said meekly.

"After the weekend we shared that was so special, I thought I meant enough to you that you would want to change your plans, so we could be together again soon," I said.

"Pam, I'm not supposed to tell anyone this, but my Top Secret Clearance is still active. You must try to forget you ever heard that," Jake said quietly.

"I don't understand what you're talking about. You've got me all confused. Surely, they must have released you from military reserve status when you were disabled."

"I can't tell you any more than that. You'll have to fill in the blanks the best you can," Jake said, looking down at the porch.

"Oh my gosh. You mean...is it dangerous? Is that why you have a gun and get the mysterious phone calls?" I asked.

Ignoring my questions, Jake said, "Pam, I will call you as soon as I know when I can tear loose. We're both aware that our mutual feelings are deeply shared. You also must know I'll be thinking about you every day." Then he reached out to give my hand a gentle squeeze. When he turned to look at me, I could have melted because I wanted him so much.

After a blissful afternoon together, Jake and I realized I had to get back on the road to the city before traffic on my end became impossible. Following a long embrace and a slow separation that seemed too painful for a mere mortal to endure, Jake carried my suitcase and travel bag out to my car. He cautioned me to be careful and wished me a safe trip as he closed the car door and leaned in to give me one last, lingering kiss.

Slowly getting up to speed, I left a trail of dust as I watched him grow smaller in my rear-view mirror. When I was back on the highway once again, I was lost in my thoughts about what could have been or should be.

Now what had I gotten myself into? I finally met my prince charming, my knight in shining armor, my soul mate, and what happened? He was not available, or at least he had other commitments. If I wasn't able to stop crying when I did, I would have had to pull over and get more tissues to see well enough to drive.

I'd only left Jake an hour before, and I missed him so much it felt like someone reached into my chest and ripped my heart out. I'd almost forgotten I had one to give and couldn't imagine that someone would want mine.

As I listened to myself, I remembered how I was going to be Ms. Big Executive with a liberated feminist ideology who was going to shatter that glass ceiling and have them all eating her dust. Been there. Done that. There was nothing else required. Where did it get me? I may have money, power, and material things, but I don't have a life.

9

I started the week off by going through the motions of my normal routines, determined to get through the day; but by Tuesday, I realized I couldn't continue to do that anymore. Try as I may, my heart just wasn't in it. Drastic action would be required on my part to initiate the necessary changes to create a life of my own, so I walked into the CEO's office and said so.

He immediately called a meeting of the Grady Board of Directors to hash out a solution. By Wednesday afternoon, they weren't very happy about what I had finally agreed to but said they could live with it if that's what I truly wanted to do. Having tried their best to change my mind, the board members said I could come back to my old position any time if I wanted to.

Wracked with indecision, I couldn't sleep and wrestled with my feelings all night long, wondering if I had made the right choice. By the dawn's early light, I realized there could be no acceptable alternative as I splashed water on my face to see if I could wake up enough to function.

With a renewed sense of purpose, I filled a suitcase with clothes and took off to beat the morning traffic up to Connecticut on the Interstate Highway.

After another long drive up from New York City, Jake answered my anxious staccato rapping of his door knocker with a bewildered look of total surprise as I threw myself into his arms. He said, "Pam! What are you doing here? It's Thursday, and I have to leave first thing tomorrow morning. I told you I'd call as soon as I knew when I could be free."

"First things first, just hug me a while longer. All I could think about since I left you is being in your arms again," I said as I showered him with kisses.

Jake said, "I missed you too, and it does feel so nice to hold you close to me again, but I don't understand what you're doing here when I have to go away for the weekend."

"Jake, after sharing what we did, I realized my whole life was a sham. I wasn't doing anything important or even what I wanted to do. I was just obsessed with making money for Grady Trading and myself. When I saw the look in Jenni's eyes while she talked about her family and the work she was doing with the Indian kids on the reservation, she was positively glowing. I knew my life didn't have the same spark or meaning. I was only going through the same motions over and over every day. So I quit."

Jake appeared to be shocked and uncertain he heard me right. "You said you quit your job after twenty years with the firm and just walked out?"

I said, "I tried, but they wouldn't let me. I told them in so many words to take the job and shove it. That I didn't want to work in New York City any longer. That I was tired of the rat race, and I wanted out. That I needed a life of my own.

"I was flabbergasted when they said they recognized how hard I worked and the long hours I put in all those years *and* it was fully appreciated! Then they said I wasn't replaceable.

"They explained how valuable they thought I was as a key player in their organization and what changes they were prepared to make to keep me available to the company. Who knew? I was really surprised to learn they felt that way. I always figured I had to keep running faster, do more, and do it better than anyone else to satisfy them. Of course, I was elated to be the object of all the hard-earned praise that was long overdue, but it didn't change how I felt.

"I spent two days negotiating a semi-retirement package. You are now looking at a telecommuter and a corporate director of Grady Trading Company. I can begin working from home at full salary and benefits, wherever home happens to be. I will select two assistants to replace me on site, and I'll delegate instead of trying to do the job all by myself. I may have to go into the city now and then, but no more than one day a week.

"Don't just stand there with your mouth gaping, Jake. I thought you'd be excited and thrilled for me. You do want me to be around here, don't you?"

"What can I say? I'm speechless. This is so sudden. It's a lot to take in all at once."

"Please tell me you're not having second thoughts about us?" I pleaded.

"No, of course not. I'm trying to absorb it all and figure out what this means in terms of me continuing to teach at Dana University in Irving and the other thing we can't discuss," Jake said.

"If you're in favor of this arrangement, I can work around your schedules. Just tell me you're as happy as I am about the prospects of us being together," I said.

"You know I'm thrilled to have you here. I just haven't figured out how all this is going to work."

"Jake, for once in your life, throw caution to the wind and live a little," I said. "Go with the flow. I just did."

"You have to be crazy. We only met a week ago. Since then you tried to quit your job and left New York because of someone you just met. I don't want you to regret a rash decision later that was made on the spur of the moment," he said.

"When I returned to the city, I left a part of me back here with you that couldn't be replaced. I'm ready to take the plunge if you are. What's the worst that can happen?"

Jake's head was churning as he tried to figure out what he would do about the work he'd been secretly doing for the CIA on his weekends and breaks at the university.

Here he had a beautiful, intelligent woman on his doorstep that he was more than attracted to. She seemed to want him as much as he wanted her. The best he could tell, they appeared to be a perfect match. He didn't want to take a chance on losing her before they got to know each other better, but where was there any time left in his life for her at the moment?

Not knowing what else he could have told her, he said, "Let's just say that I'm in a delicate phase of something this weekend, and I don't know where it will end up. I can't just walk away. There are too many things to be considered and potential repercussions. We can talk about this more when I get back Sunday night, but what will you do here all weekend by yourself?"

"I have everything I need in my laptop to keep me busy while I work out the details of my new position. Why don't we just celebrate finding each other and being back together again."

"What kind of celebration did you have in mind?" Jake asked, raising one eyebrow inquisitively.

"How about we go skinny dipping again while we still have most of the full moon left? Then we can come in and spend the night in front of the fireplace," I said.

"There's nothing I'd like more than to be with you, but I hope you're sure this is what you want to do," Jake replied.

"I've only been able to think about you and us being together all week. Now are we going take that celebratory 'swim' or not?" I said, not willing to settle for anything less.

"Okay, but I have to pack and leave bright and early in the morning."

"Now you're talking! I'll race you to the dock. Last one in is a rotten egg," I yelled over my shoulder as I slammed the door behind me.

Jake yanked the door open only to see the trail of clothes I left behind on my way to the water. He struggled to unbutton his shirt with one hand as he closed the door with the other.

He must have heard me splash into the pond.

"I hope that wasn't a belly flop, and you didn't hurt yourself." Jake yelled, trying to be quiet.

Jake sounded like he was really concerned because he couldn't see me in the dark while still trying to remove his pants and shoes. He called my name when he ran into the water, but I sprang up from where I was watching him from under the dock.

"Pam! Don't ever scare me like that again," he said, looking really concerned.

"Jake, I've waited all week so we could be together again like this. Hold me close and never let me go."

He reeled when I climbed all over him, smothering him with kisses, his muscles rippling as he tried to keep us both from falling into the water. The moon reappeared from behind the clouds as he picked me up and carefully deposited me on the dock as if I were a fragile flower. His eyes shone in the moonlight as he pushed my wet hair aside, nibbled on my neck and slowly worked his way down to my breasts. "Did I mention how absolutely delicious you look in the moonlight?" He asked out of the side of his mouth with my right nipple fully engaged while he was gently caressing the other. Not waiting for an answer, he proceeded to kiss and massage me all over.

I rolled off the dock and grabbed Jake around his shoulders. "Come here," I insisted. "Oh, how I've missed you so. I've never felt this horny or wanted anyone this much before." I slid into place and locked my legs behind him. "That's it. Deeper," I commanded in a throaty voice even I didn't recognize as my own while digging my nails into Jake's back.

Without stopping, Jake slowly eased his way further into the water where both of us could move more freely. For a split second, I left my state of euphoria and started to panic when I wondered if our actions would bother Jake's back. Then I realized the buoyancy of the water must have been relieving the pressure on his spine since he appeared to be enjoying it as much as I was. Because he continued without missing a beat, I was certain of it.

Once we slowed down the frantic tempo, we seemed to reach an equally shared state of bliss that didn't abate. The gentle waves driven by the warm night breezes lapped the shore in rhythm with our movements. I couldn't believe Jake's staying power as I drifted into wave after wave of ecstasy.

I was astonished the attraction and intensity of our lovemaking appeared to be mutual. We couldn't seem to get enough of each other, perhaps because of the pleasures we've both denied ourselves through the years. Maybe we never did meet the right partner at the right time.

When we were both totally spent, Jake carried me back to the house, past the trail of clothes we left behind in the rush to get to the pond. He was still kissing me as he fumbled with the doorknob, kicked the door closed, and swung my feet at a pair of throw pillows on the couch to knock them down to the floor in front of the fire. Without a pause, he laid me down with my head on a pillow, flipped the switch on the gas log fireplace, and snuggled up close to me on the rug.

I said, “I was dreaming about being with you again all week, but tonight was infinitely better than I possibly could have ever imagined. Where have you been all my life?”

“What we just shared was absolutely fantastic, but I have to leave first thing in the morning, and I’m not even packed yet. If you keep this up, I’ll never want to leave, and then I’ll be in big trouble with the government,” Jake said.

“Okay, maybe I should have called, but I wanted to surprise you, and I couldn’t wait to get here to tell you the good news. Tell you what, I’ll go outside and round up our clothes while you pack, and we’ll set the alarm clock in time for you to get up in case either one of us manages to get any sleep tonight,” I said.

10

I saw Jake pull into the garage after being away for three days, and I rushed out to greet him. "Hi, honey. I'm so glad that you're finally home. I've missed you so much. I couldn't wait for the weekend to be over so we could be together again. Did everything go as planned?" I said in rapid succession.

"Yes, everything went as well as could be expected, and I missed you too."

After many breathless, prolonged kisses, we stumbled into the house, afraid to break our physical connection; I inhaled deeply, gasping for air. "Wow! Being in your arms was all I could think about while you were gone. I thought the long weekend would never get over, so we could be together again.

"I'm sorry, you must be tired. Is there anything I can get for you? Beer, coffee, tea, me?" I asked hopefully with a big smile.

Flopping into a kitchen chair, Jake replied, "I am exhausted and parched from hiking through brush and briars all day. A cold beer would be great about now."

I was all wound up after being alone for three days and resumed talking nonstop on the way to the refrigerator, "I hope you don't mind, but I bought a few curtains and blinds, so we can have a little privacy in your bachelor pad. Do you like them?"

"They look very nice and add a finished touch to the windows," Jake said. "If you had waited, I could have helped you install them though."

"I was in a rush because I wanted to surprise you. After I smashed my finger with the hammer trying to put up the brackets, I had trouble finding the Band-aids. Never would have thought to look in your toolbox, but I came across them when I was looking for a Phillips screwdriver in your garage. I was surprised to find yet another handgun and a box of bullets in your toolbox. Just how dangerous is the work you're doing for the government?" I asked, concerned.

Hesitating for a second or two as if distracted, Jake said, "It's just a backup, nothing to worry about."

"I bought a bottle of Johannesburg Riesling wine to go with a DiGiorno three meat rising crust pizza. The oven is already preheated, so dinner will be ready in about thirty minutes. I'm not a great cook, but I can learn. I hate to be such a chatterbox, but I am so anxious to share everything with you." I said, wondering what could be on Jake's mind.

Jake stood, took the beer and mug from my hands, set them on the table, looked at me with those gorgeous blue eyes, smiled, and said, "Whoa, slow down. I'm not going anywhere. There's no rush. Come here and give me another big hug and a kiss."

Following a long embrace and a kiss that didn't seem to have an ending, he stepped back and said, "I'm all hot and sweaty from the trip. I hope I didn't give you a beard burn. You can throw the pizza in the oven now if you want to while I shave and shower. I have worked up a big appetite after an exceptionally hectic weekend without taking enough time to eat."

"I'll put the pizza in the oven and drop the temperature, so it'll cook nice and slow while we take a long shower together. If you trust me, I can shave you in the shower. We'll be able to tell when the pizza is done because the cheese will be melted."

"And how do you know that, Ms. 'I don't know how to cook, but I can learn'?" Jake asked, as he grinned and gave me a peck on the lips.

"Jake, really! It says right in the instructions, 'The pizza is done when the cheese is melted and the crust is a golden brown.' Now let's go get you showered and shaved."

We lingered in the shower to make up for lost time, having been apart for three days.

Following our resplendent but leisurely shower together, I retrieved a pair of long stemmed glasses I had chilling in the freezer, uncorked the bottle, and poured the wine.

Checking the pizza in the oven, Jake looked surprised to see the pizza was done to perfection, considering how long we were in the shower. The crust was nicely browned, and the cheese was fully melted. He removed the pizza from the oven, and I found the cutter in the junk drawer. Jake sliced the pizza in short order and brought it to the table.

He went into the living room to put on some romantic music as I lit the candles to set the mood. We sat down at the same time, raised our glasses and clunked them together as Jake said, "To us, may we always be together."

I reached out for Jake's hand, looked into his eyes at the reflection of the flickering candlelight, and wondered if it could possibly get any better. How could I have ever thought that any position in the executive suite was worth more than this?

When the mozzarella cheese on the pizza cooled enough to eat, Jake scoffed down a large piece. He wondered how a fantastic girl like Pam could pop into his life out of nowhere, but instead of telling her that, he proclaimed, "Pam, this has to be the best frozen pizza I've ever had. Good choice."

"By the way, I almost forgot to mention I had to tell the government we are involved. They'll have to do a background check on you, but they assured me that it would be done very discreetly."

"Jake, this sounds like it could get spooky. What if I don't pass muster?" I asked.

"Don't be silly. There'll be no problem unless you've been selling national security secrets to the Chinese and Russians," Jake said.

He was ravenous, not having had much opportunity to eat over the long weekend. After gobbling up four pieces of pizza to my two, he dragged me into the living room, flipped the switch on the gas log flame, and went back to the kitchen to retrieve the rest of the wine. Returning to the living room, he found the lights out and me, hopefully looking absolutely adorable, wearing nothing but a smile in the warm flickering glow of the fireplace.

I patted the rug next to me to show Jake where he should park himself. We made love tenderly as we polished off the rest of the wine before heading for the bedroom, hand in hand. We resumed making up for all the time lost over the weekend, which seemed much, much too long because we no longer wanted to be apart.

After spending another wonderful night of heavenly bliss together, I fixed a nourishing breakfast of scrambled eggs, sausages, orange juice, wheat toast, and coffee. Jake filled his briefcase, gave me a big smooch, and rushed off to lecture at DUI.

Jake's instructors had given the test to his lecture class for him on Friday while he was away. There were only a few students on the track team with an out of town meet who had to take a makeup exam upon his return. At the end of the day, his mind kept straying back to Pam as he tried to focus at the monthly staff meeting.

He was so anxious to get home that he almost didn't see the state cruiser as he rounded the corner, but he slowed down just in time without making it seem too obvious. Being careful to concentrate on his driving the rest of the way, he saw Pam waiting for him on the front porch with a book in her lap as he slowly pulled in the driveway. Jake is once again taken aback by the vision of her beauty, her golden hair softly illuminated to a rose tone by the low angle of the waning sunlight that it almost took his breath away.

"Hi, Jake. Welcome home. How did your first day back at school go after the weekend away?" I asked.

"Hi, sweetie. Not bad," Jake replied. "The instructors gave the exam I left with them. I just have to grade the test papers and the lab reports tonight. I heard about the preliminary results of your background check. They said because of your international financial experience and contacts, they want to discuss the possibility of you doing a little investigating for them from time to time."

"They said. Who said?" I asked, surprised.

"I guess I can tell you this much. It's the CIA. They will contact you when they're ready." Jake said.

"Is that who you've been doing this clandestine cloak and dagger stuff for?"

"I still can't tell you anything about that yet. Not until or unless you are issued a final security clearance," Jake said.

After a quick meal, Jake graded the papers from the previous Friday's quiz and lab reports on the arm of the couch while I laid my head on his lap. As soon as he finished, we wandered off to the bedroom to recuperate after all the delightful time we've shared since I showed up on his doorstep the previous Thursday.

With a good night's sleep, the next day went much easier when he could focus on the details of his position at DUI. As he drove home this time, he paid more attention to the speed limit. "Hi, cutie. You are starting to become habit forming," he said. "It's getting so I daydream about you intermittently throughout the day, and I'm losing concentration in the middle of my lectures. I can't wait for the end of the classes to come home to be with you again either."

I said, "Just as long as you're not distracted by all those young, voluptuous women on campus and in your lecture hall. I want to keep you all to myself. Speaking of our time together, I had a couple of guys drop by today in a big, black SUV. They looked like they should have been wearing trench coats.

After spending the afternoon interviewing me, they wanted to know how soon I could start doing work on a project. They waved the flag and talked about doing it for country, motherhood, and apple pie, but I said I'd have to think it over and get back to them."

"So, do you know what you want to do about it?" Jake inquired as he wrapped his arms around me.

"They had no idea how much time on my part would be involved. It would vary immensely by assignment. I told them I left New York to be with you and didn't want to be tied up that much or have to keep making trips to New York on business or Langley for them."

"How would you feel about being tied up by me?" Jake asked with a sly grin. "I could use silk scarves to avoid leaving any marks."

As I looked into those deep blue eyes, I exclaimed, "That's the best idea I've heard all day! It's a little kinky and totally unnecessary though. You know I can be very cooperative, and I'd follow your instructions to the letter. It might be good practice in case I were captured behind enemy lines and tortured. That is, unless I were caught and taken prisoner by you. I'd tell you anything you wanted to know or hear, just so you wouldn't stop."

Jake said, "If you keep talking that way, I'll throw you on the bed and have my way with you."

I moved even closer, reached up to put my arms around his neck, and said with a slinky voice, "Are you sure it isn't my turn to be in charge? I thought we were supposed to use the rug in the den next. You know what they say, sticks and stones may break my bones, but whips and chains excite me."

"Is it possible that you could be turning into a sex addict?" Jake asked. "You seem to become more aggressive with each passing day, if that's possible."

"The only thing I'm addicted to is you, babe, and I like it. Thank you so much for being you. This is much better than sitting home alone in my New York apartment pouring over financial reports. I'm so happy to be here, sharing everything together. Moving in with you was the best decision I've ever made. Do you feel the same way?" I asked.

"You blew into my life like a whirlwind. I didn't know what hit me. My only regret is that we didn't meet up sooner, but maybe you wouldn't have been ready to chuck everything you'd worked so hard for in the city and move here," Jake said.

We eventually settled down to a more sustainable, less anxious pace of doing things. We learned to savor each moment together without the implied fear that everything could evaporate and we might wake from our wondrous dream.

11

One evening after dinner, Jake looked up at me from the papers he was grading. "Well it's been a week. Have you decided if you want to be a spy or not?" he asked.

"I've been kind of waiting to see how the office would operate without me being there all the time. Even with temps filling in, it's not falling apart. I'm able to keep track of everything that's going on from here. I think it will work out fine once we get the permanent people on board.

"That got me to thinking about the government's quandary. They claim they need my expertise, but I don't want another time drain at this point in my life. So I said to myself, 'Self, why don't I consult for them instead? If they can define their problems, I can tell them where to go, what to look for, and what they can do with the information. Then they do all the leg work, and I keep my legs where I want them to be.' Does that sound like a great approach or what?" I asked.

Jake replied, "It's little wonder they promoted you to vice president in the first place. Grady Trading Company was also smart enough to give you what you wanted when you tried to leave, so you'd still be available for them. Maybe someone in government is that bright as well. Give it a shot.

What have you got to lose? They can always say no, and if you don't like any counterproposals forthcoming, you can decline those as well."

"That's what I thought too, but another thing occurred to me as well, Jake. Are your extracurricular assignments slowing down, or will they be ongoing? I worry that you might end up in harm's way, and I don't want to share you with Uncle Sam forever you know. At some point, I want to have you all to myself."

"I can't say that there is no risk or promise anything about duration, but it would appear there's a light at the end of the tunnel. It's possible it might taper off soon. I told them I may want to ease out of the program, so they should find a replacement I could train for the team," Jake said.

"Jake, we both paid our dues and need simpler lives to enjoy our time together. I'll tell the G-men I can help them out in an advisory capacity on a couple of assignments on a short term, trial basis."

Another week elapsed without word from the CIA. Finally, Taylor Young called to inform me that my security clearance had been approved, and they wanted to meet that evening.

When Jake showed up after work, I said, "I know you put in a long day, darling, but I got a call from the agents. They'd like to meet us tonight at the parking lot of Friendly's Ice Cream in Wilbraham. We'll have to take my Cadillac because they will ride with us to the Springfield Symphony Orchestra concert at Stanley Park in Westfield. They'll bring special lawn chairs equipped with multidirectional frequency jammers. It will be with your contact agent, Manny Rodriquez, and he's bringing a woman named Taylor Young."

"And why would I be involved?" Jake asked.

I explained to Jake that the CIA didn't want to raise suspicions by showing up at our house again or take a chance of having anyone follow me home from their local office. "She told me not to write any of this down, so I'll see if I can remember it all. You'll sit in the back of the car and pretend that Taylor is your date. Manny will sit up front with me. A couple of other units will monitor our progress to make sure we're not being followed. They said that what they want to discuss is very sensitive and may have international and political repercussions."

"They will bring a short range audio amplifier earpiece, so I could hear what they are whispering with their throat mikes. We'll sit toward the back of the audience in the middle to block any parabolic listening devices. Because the evening is warm, fan yourself with the program. Make sure your mouth is covered with the program if you say anything at all, so no one can read your lips. I'll be sitting between them, and you'll be sitting on the other side of Taylor, since you're supposed to be together. You won't be included in the conversation, but Taylor will talk to you now and then to make it look normal. You're supposed to act like you are having a good time. Do you have all that?"

Jake replied, "Boy Pam, things have changed since 911. I never had to go through all of this before when I was recruited by the CIA. I'm beginning to be sorry I got you involved. The last thing I wanted to do was to make your life more complicated or put you in harm's way."

I turned to look at Jake and said, "This sounds exciting, and it could be fun. They said you should wear shorts and a polo shirt, so we look like we're dressed appropriately for the weather."

Jake changed out of his suit and hurried to get ready. We reached the designated meeting place on time where the agents were already waiting for us. Our drive to Stanley Park in Westfield on the Massachusetts Turnpike was uneventful.

We helped the agents carry the chairs and the picnic basket they'd brought along. Then they set up the specially equipped lawn chairs, which were activated with a remote hidden in Taylor's purse. I was surprised at the size of the pistol she could fit in there too. It looked to be much bigger than her small hands could handle.

Once situated in the crowd, we all dug into the sandwiches Manny had picked up at a Subway restaurant while we discussed the game plan.

Jake was impressed with the orchestra's repertoire and precision but only half listened to the music because of his concerns for Pam's well-being.

With the reduced highway traffic after the evening concert, I drove back on US Route 20 through the Springfields, dropping Taylor and Manny off at their car in Wilbraham.

Once we were on our way home, Jake said, "I was only along for the ride, so I tried not to listen. Can you give me the gist of what they want you to do?"

"According to them, we can discuss generalities since you have a top secret security clearance, but we should avoid discussing too many specifics. Basically, they want me to help them learn how to find and follow the electronic money trails and the complex series of financial wire transfers the Iranians and other Arab countries use to hide the oil money earmarked for financing the radical jihadists.

"The CIA hasn't been able to keep up with the international trend of shifting banking centers from Switzerland and offshore islands to Hong Kong and Singapore to shelter money from taxes. The Ugland House on the Cayman Islands has become too loose with information on their clients for oil money laundering and to remain an effective tax haven. The CIA also needs to be able to track money flow from places like Iran to the terrorists' networks to predict where the next major strikes might come from. "The United States has lost track of most of the Chinese, Muslim extremists, and North Koreans we let flood the country that have become embedded in our communities. The theft of technology by them and third world countries has seriously damaged our economy. Many of these foreign nationals have become US citizens, working for our government and primary weapon system contractors. We don't know about block payments to the sheltered accounts of their spies when the amounts don't trigger the $10,000 reporting requirement here.

"I agreed to supply international contact information only in person to a single designated liaison. They cannot reveal what led our agents to contact them. That way there wouldn't be an electronic or paper trail. Then the information can't be traced back to me or my firm.

"They did tell me they left a confidential operational procedures manual in the trunk of my car when they were taking their electronic lawn chairs out. I'm to review their methods and recommend improvements where I can."

"I don't know about this, Pam. I hope these government agents are better at keeping secrets than the Watergate plumbers and the State Department people involved in the Benghazi cover-up. I've been worried about your safety since this whole thing arose."

"How is this any different than the work you are doing for the government?" I kind of like the prospects of being able to do something that will help round up some of the people who threaten our country. I wonder if I can get an undercover name? How does *The Money Whisperer* sound to you?"

"The only place I want you doing undercover work is in our bedroom. Then you can whisper sweet nothings in my ear all you want," Jake said as he reached over to hold my free hand.

"Okay, I showed you mine, now you show me yours,"

I said.

"I thought you had seen all of me before this point in time. Now you want me to show you my what, exactly?" Jake asked with a bewildered look.

"I told you what the CIA wants me to do. Now that my security clearance has been approved, you can tell me what sort of mysterious things you and Manny have been doing out at the Quabbin Reservoir. Not knowing only makes me worry that much more because of all the things I imagine that could happen to you out there in the wilderness."

Jake thought for a moment and explained, "Well, actually Manny is the facilitator and doesn't go out into the field. After trace quantities of toxic chemicals turned up intermittently in routine quality control testing of Boston's tap water, I was asked to assemble a task force to locate the source of contaminates and identify the culprits poisoning the water supply for the greater Boston area.

"My team goes out in the evenings and on weekends posing as hunters, wildlife photographers, and fishermen, depending on the season. We look for the bad guys and take water samples from different locations. I have blind samples analyzed by my graduate students for extra credit. They don't know where the samples come from or what they're looking for. I sent the reports to Manny at Langley along with the locations sampled as the grids are filled in.

I might have to deal with some of these bad guys face to face, but I've been trained for that. Hopefully, you will never have to encounter any of them."

"Jake, why didn't you tell me all about this before? Have you run into any terrorists at the Quabbin Reservoir?" I wanted to know.

"I couldn't tell you anything until your security clearance was approved, Pam. I also was reluctant to worry you unnecessarily," Jake said.

"And... have you run into any bad guys, as you call them," I asked.

"That has only happened once so far. Did you read in the newspapers about the chemical engineers from Pakistan, Saudi Arabia, and Singapore apprehended at the Quabbin earlier this year?" Jake asked.

"Yes, I did. What has that got to do with you, Jake?"

"That was my Quabbin Task Force Team that apprehended them prowling around the Goodnough Dike long after closing hours. They claimed to be studying the reservoir system," Jake said.

"I caught the one that tried to make a break for it. That's why I was still sore on the weekend we met. We tumbled down the hill when I tackled him. Since we were supposed to be keeping a low profile, we turned them over to the Massachusetts State Police. The police found out they were Muslins, but without any proof they were up to no good, they were all released since the only thing they could be charged with was trespassing after dark. Now you know as much about it as I can tell you," Jake said.

"I'm glad you told me, but I don't see how I could be in any danger by doing research for the CIA," I said.

"That reminds me, I didn't check the police arrest reports to make sure the names of my task force were removed. Now that I think about it, the guy that was watching us on the train might have been one of them. I thought he looked a little familiar. Maybe that's where they got my name from, but I can't imagine why he'd want to follow me." Jake said.

"That doesn't sound as bad as I imagined. You were fortunate they weren't carrying weapons. Please try to be careful," I said as I made the last turn into the driveway. We trudged into the house, lost in our own thoughts about the day's chain of events, and got ready for bed. We were both tired from the mental gymnastics of keeping up with all the conversations of the evening. We snuggle up together and were soon fast asleep in each other's arms.

12

Fully rested after a good night's sleep, Jake breezed through his lectures and the supervision of his students' lab experiments. Jake was preoccupied with conflicting emotions of being glad to finally have the CIA task definition resolved for Pam, yet he was still concerned about the potential danger in her assignments. Then a professor down the hall approached him with a pleasant surprise that granted him a respite from his quandary.

He arrived home with renewed energy, bounded through the door, and said, "Hi, Pam, do we have any plans for tonight? One of the guys in the chemistry department had a couple of tickets to a Neil Diamond concert that he can't use. It's at eight tonight in the MassMutual Center."

"That sounds great. I love Neil Diamond. Unfortunately, the last time I went to see him live, I almost went deaf because the volume was so loud. I thought the bass speakers were going to rattle my rib cage loose. I hope the seats are at least in the back of the balcony this time.

I only have to slip into a dress and put my face on. I'll be ready in about fifteen minutes. If you're hungry, you can heat up something from the doggie bag we took home from our meal at the Villa Rose Restaurant last night while I change."

After getting off the interstate highway ramp onto downtown Springfield's maze of streets, I said, "Did you happen to see the big, black SUV following us about four cars back? I couldn't help but notice the extra antennas mounted on the back. Maybe it's my imagination, but it mirrored the last few turns we took."

Jake said, "It could be someone going to the same concert or another event in downtown Springfield. It's probably just a coincidence they are going the same route we are."

We ended up in the wrong lane to catch the turn at the municipal parking garage but lucked out finding an empty parking space on a side street around the corner. Looking around, we didn't see the oversized SUV, so we went into the MassMutual Center.

The seats were not too close to the stage, and the volume wasn't so loud this time as we settled in for a relaxing evening of delightful music we both happen to prefer. We were far from being disappointed by Neil Diamond's selections of his oldies we grew up with.

On the way out to the truck, I said, "That was a great concert. Neil seemed to have a problem with his voice at the last performance of his I went to. Then he had to rely more on a backup singer for reinforcement. His tones seemed to be much fuller and richer this time, so maybe he has been giving fewer concerts since then."

Jake signaled for a left turn, but as I watched for a break in the line of oncoming traffic, I happened to look in the rearview mirror. "Uh-oh, there's that black SUV again with all those aerials. He's three cars back. Can you try to lose him?"

"I'll see what I can do. It shouldn't be difficult with all these traffic signals," Jake said as he darted in between the stream of the oncoming traffic to get through the intersection.

After a few last minute turns while running red lights, Jake said, "It looks like I lost him. Do you suppose the Feds had somebody tailing us for our protection?"

I said, "They never mentioned anything about that. I'll ask the next time we have a meeting."

We arrived home without incident and had a good night's sleep. When Jake called home the next day, he said he didn't notice anything unusual as he went through his daily routine at the university. I went out to run my errands before meeting Taylor Young at a prearranged location.

When Jake arrived home that evening, I said, "Jake, I saw Taylor today. It was the CIA that was tailing us. I sure gave her an earful. I read her the riot act for doing that without telling us. I said that under no circumstances are they to ever do that again unless we ask for help. She claimed it was standard procedure with a new field operative. I explained that the deal was that I would consult, but there was no way I would become an operative. She said she'd get back to me on that once she talked to her superiors."

A couple of days passed as Jake and I settled into a routine. Jake would go off to lecture and cover both the laboratory experiments and the pilot plant facility while I kept track of the Grady Trading Company on the computer and by phone.

"So how are things going in New York at GTC without you being there to lead the charge on a daily basis?" Jake asked one evening.

"Surprisingly well," I replied. "Maybe I wasn't as indispensable as I thought. It's remarkable that the two new permanent people I hired were both quick studies and able to follow directions in detail. I guess my gut feelings about them during the interview process were right on target. All those years I felt I had to do everything all by myself to have it done right, when I could have been delegating assignments instead. It's going so smoothly; I may not even have to go down there once a week. If I knew what else I could do at this point in my life, I might even consider taking complete early retirement and starting over at something else."

"We both know you needed the experience of that time in the saddle to learn the ropes and make the right judgment calls," Jake said. "Now you're a seasoned pro and can operate your office efficiently from at least four highway hours away. Even though those two rookies have long lists of experience in the business on their resumes, I'm sure they couldn't be as productive if you weren't available to guide them. If you think back, I'll bet you were overwhelmed when you first started there. Being female in a man's world at the time, I suspect nobody took you under their wing or even offered any help at all."

"Yeah, I guess you're right. Maybe I am smarter than the average bear. If my arm was longer, I could give myself a pat on the back," I said with a grin.

Jake turned and said, "I have a suggestion. Have you ever considered teaching at the college level? The school of business management here at the university would be thrilled to have someone with your experience and capabilities. It wouldn't pay anything close to what you're accustomed to earning, but you could also remain on the board of directors at Grady Trading Company.

When I was in undergraduate school, we learned the most from the engineering professors who had industrial experience. Most of the others had never ventured out beyond the world of academia because they couldn't see the need to relate to the real world. It was not so much because they only stayed in the relative safety of their ivory towers with their tenure. They had never been challenged to solve real time practical problems in the business community and couldn't make the same contributions in class. I had more opportunities to make positive financial impacts on commercial operations than they did even as an undergrad on my summer jobs in the chemical industry."

"Jake, what a great idea. I hadn't thought of that. Jenni Blackfoot finds teaching at the Indian reservation so rewarding. I could give back with my experience in business. Maybe I'll consider it. Who is the dean of the DUI Business School in case I have questions or decide to initiate a conversation?"

"She would be Jan Brytowski. It's extension 200 off the main number. I just had to call her about a student who had a unit operations lab experiment that conflicted with an exam in her department. We worked the scheduling out," Jake said.

After dinner, we leisurely strolled down to the edge of the water, and I commented, "I noticed the houses here seem to be spaced evenly around the pond. Does that mean the road goes all the way through if we wanted to do a walkabout?"

"Yeah, as a matter of fact I should be getting more exercise. My physical therapist gets impatient with me when I tell him I don't use the treadmill in the garage in between my sessions there. Would you care to circumnavigate the pond now?" Jake asked.

"I'm ready when you are," I said. "I should find a local gym up here to work out too. I've really been slacking off since I left the city."

"Okay, let's go. I don't know many of the neighbors on the far side, but we can always introduce ourselves if they're out and about," Jake said.

"Are they going to say, 'We didn't recognize you two with your clothes on'?"

"No worries, mate. I'm sure any image they manage to capture with their infrared, telescopic, night vision lens would be totally blurred at that distance. The pictures obtained definitely wouldn't be of sufficient quality for publication in any respectable magazine. Although with your body, I could hardly blame any scandal sheet for printing your picture in the altogether regardless of the clarity," Jake said.

"Since you're into old songs, darling, do you remember a number by Sheena Easton called, 'For Your Eyes Only'?" I asked.

"Have you been going through my old albums? That happens to be another of my favorites. The melody is absolutely haunting. It's been so long since I played it; I'd almost forgotten I still had it," Jake said.

"My message is the same as the title, 'For Your Eyes Only,' love. After all those years in New York, I'm not as shy as I once was, but I draw the line at sharing with anyone but you," I said.

"Message received and duly noted. If I haven't conveyed how much I appreciate your acts of sharing often enough, please let me know. By the way, is that a snake over there?" Jake said.

"What snake! Where?" I screamed.

"Oh, it's only a crooked stick. Sorry. Your reaction time is really impressive though. Do you think you could let go of my arm now? You may be cutting off the circulation," Jake said.

"Don't you dare frighten me like that again, Jacob Wells. I'm finally beginning to fully relax and look forward to our skinny dipping sessions on these warm nights. I don't want to have to be on the lookout for strange critters lurking about. I still think I had a fish nibbling on me the last time," I said.

"Boy, it sure is a beautiful day. We should make a point to do this several times a week. Exercising is a lot more fun when I can share it with you."

"Is it fun even with our clothes on in the daytime?" I asked.

Jake said, "Even then. Although the advantage at the moment is that we can understand what is being said without all the heavy breathing."

"So, we should be walking faster then?" I asked.

Following an enjoyable walk at a respectable pace, we retired to the cottage. I picked up a book by Danielle Steel I'd been reading, and Jake was organizing his paperwork for classes the following day. When he finished, we happened to both look up at the same time. Although we had settled into a more laid back, relaxed attitude when we were together, none of the fire and intense passion between us had diminished. Not a word needed to be spoken as we simultaneously walked toward the bedroom and slowly began to undress each other...

13

The following day, Jake arrived home a little earlier than usual. I said, "Hi, hon. I'm glad you're here. I wanted to tell you I called Dean Brytowski today to explore possibilities of teaching in the DUI School of Business. I told her I didn't have an up-to-date resume prepared, but she insisted we meet for lunch anyway.

"It so happens she does have a staff opening for the fall semester. She was thrilled to consider someone with my Wall Street experience. Bottom line is that we hit it off exceptionally well. I suspect the position is mine if I want it."

Jake said, "That's great news if it's what you decide you want to do. Why are you grinning as if there's something else?"

"Well, when I got back, I called Raymond Page, the chairman of the board at GTC. He was pleased with what he's been hearing about the performance of my department, even since I left to telecommute. It didn't seem to bother him if I were to retire, except from the board of directors' position. He just wants to know I'll be available to help guide the firm through major financial decisions and over any unforeseen hurdles down the road.

"He proposed we fly from Bradley-Hartford to JFK airport for dinner tomorrow night in New York. He'll arrange to have us picked up, and we'll stay over the weekend at the Airport Hilton Double Tree Hotel. He'd like us to meet with the upper management team to discuss all the variables, potential repercussions, and possible worse case scenarios if I were to leave. I told him I'd have to talk it over with you and let him know. What do you think?"

"It's your decision, Pam. It's a big step breaking away from everything you've worked so hard to achieve over your whole career. Are you absolutely positive you want to consider doing this? There may be no turning back," Jake said.

I said, "That depends on you. Do you want to put up with me forever and ever?"

"Honey, I'd be delighted," Jake replied. "There's nothing I'd like more, but I should reiterate, we have a very short history together. Could this be another hasty decision along the way? Do you think you know me well enough to decide now, or do you want to think about it a while and see what happens over time?"

"I'm already convinced I know who you are, who we are, and how I want us to spend the rest of our lives together. It was making a commitment that involved you I was concerned about. I'll call and have them make the arrangements for the weekend. Did I mention I'm beginning to like you a whole lot?"

The rest of the week seemed to fly by as I apparently became more upbeat in my mood and outlook. Perhaps being enthused about turning the page to start a completely new chapter in my life, finalizing my direction toward a new career, and being able to share everything with Jake meant more to me than I had realized. Maybe I did have my head in the sand all those years while life passed me by. I guess I was too busy keeping the company afloat, without regard for carving out a niche for myself. I suspect having Jake by my side showed me just how wonderful life can really be.

The weekend was finally upon us. As we approached Bradley International Airport, I was once again torn between leaving the city, in charge of transferring millions of dollars in funds from one account and location to another or being with my first real love and soul mate to live happily ever after.

When I sorted it out that way in my mind, there was no contest. The power and prestige of being in charge, left to my own wits to survive in the world of business couldn't hold a candle to sharing a life with my true love as an equal partner.

After a short hop from Hartford, we ended up circling JFK for forty-five minutes while waiting for the overseas and transcontinental flights to land since they were low on fuel. At last we were given final runway approach clearance, and the fasten seatbelts light came on. I turned to look at Jake, and my heart became one big ball of mush because I'd grown to love him so much more with each passing day.

Jake caught me looking at him, and a smile lit up his face. He said, "I can't believe I've found someone that's such a perfect match for me in every way," as he gave me a peck on the cheek and squeezed my hand.

With only light carry-on luggage for the weekend, we deplaned and saw a limo driver holding up a sign with P. MULLEN–GTC in large block letters as we walked out of the gate area. After a short ride to the nearby Double Tree Hilton, we were led up to a large conference room where the full board of directors and the principle officers of Grady Trading awaited our arrival. Everyone stood to greet me with applause as the guest of honor upon our entry, but I gestured for them to sit down, trying not to be embarrassed with all the attention aimed in my direction.

After finding our spot reserved at the head of the table, I introduced Jake to Raymond Page, chairman of the board before we sat down. Ray remained standing and noted that on this occasion he couldn't be politically correct because of all I had done for the company to instill the growth Grady had enjoyed with me at the financial tiller. He added that they'd missed having their beauty with a brain on company premises but was confident that everyone present, without exception, wished me the best of everything in the future. Then he gave me a great big bear hug while he whispered to Jake that he'd better take good care of me, or else.

I said thank you to Raymond and no offense taken. Then I told the group I wasn't expecting all of this and introduced Jacob Wells, professor at Dana University in Irving. I mentioned I'd still be available to answer any questions by e-mail or phone and at board meetings.

During dinner, Raymond suggested we probably could use a respite from our trip and mentioned they only had a short agenda to address a few issues in the Grady business meeting to follow.

After the meeting and too many handshakes, hugs and good-byes, we were shown to our suite where we hibernated like a couple of love struck honeymooners for the rest of the weekend, subsisting on whatever looked interesting on the room service menu. We looked around and wondered why we bothered to pack any clothes for the trip. The luggage hadn't been touched since we entered the room. Jake said the hotel robes were comfortable, because he'd used one each time he answered the door for room service.

Once we returned to JFK airport and boarded the plane for the trip back to Hartford, I said, "Well, that was one heck of a weekend, Jake. I'm glad my arrangements with GTC have been finalized. It felt a little strange walking away from the only employer I've ever had and being in limbo for a while.

"Staying in a luxury hotel together was certainly different for us than our first night in the Best Western Motel in Lennox. The Hilton Romance Package with the full American, in-room breakfast really was really special because I didn't have to run off to any business meetings *and* I had you there with me. Do you suppose we should install a Jacuzzi at home like the one in our room at the Hilton?"

"I don't know about that. If we had a hot tub outside, would you really want to roll in the snow afterward?" Jake asked.

14

After we were back home for a few days and settled into the groove, Jake said over coffee one evening, "I turned down my usual summer industrial employment offer at Monsanto this year. The government still hasn't gotten back to me on where my undercover work is headed either, and I want to spend more time with you. What do you think about going on vacation for the summer?"

"Where did you have in mind?" I asked.

"I was thinking about a little cooler climate than the summer here, in a place where they speak English fluently. How about Canada or the United Kingdom? That's unless there's somewhere else you'd rather go."

"No, either place would be fine. The thought of taking a personal vacation after all these years is kind of exciting. Especially if it's with you," I said, batting my baby blues.

"We should both check with our government contacts to see if there's a problem with us leaving the country for a while," Jake said.

The next day, I got a return call from the CIA and told Jake, "Taylor said they have no problem with us going to Canada or the UK. They did want to know if I could intercede on a few sensitive transactions for them with my old contacts in London's Financial District if we do end up there. They struck out with making a connection between the referrals I provided in Asia and the Iranians."

"Is there any possible danger to you involved?" Jake inquired with a frown.

"They said no, but they will have us under surveillance to make sure nobody is following us while we're in the Canary Warf section of London. Then we'll be on our own for our first vacation together." I said with a big grin.

"I'd like to see if we can't do a little genealogy tracing while we're over there," Jake said. "The name Wells is an occupational name derived from the Wellman who was responsible for the village spring.

I looked up Mullen too. Some Mullens were Irish and Scottish, but the English version was derived from the French word for mill. Maybe we can dig up a few of your predecessors while we're over there. I don't know if we could get your great, great, great Uncle Angus MacMullen to clear customs without papers on the way home though."

I bristled at the thought of exhuming any of my ancient ancestors and bringing them to the new world. Then I asked Jake, "Do you know you really have a weird sense of humor?"

Jake responded, "No, but hum a few bars. Maybe I can pick up the melody."

After calming down, I got in touch with my counterparts in the United Kingdom using my Grady Trading Company credentials. Deciding Barclays Bank would have the broadest number of contacts in Asia, I sent a detailed list of requirements to an old friend there. By dispatching my request via courier through the US State Department, it would have appeared to have arrived through the normal mail. I finalized the rest of the arrangements with Taylor at the CIA.

Jake was able to find a temporary replacement for him on the task force with Manny's blessings, so he could take a sabbatical for the summer from being a weekend warrior as long as he stayed in touch. I made the reservations at a company discount and upgraded our seating with my frequent flier miles after coordinating with Barclays Bank in London.

15

The day of departure arrived at last, and Jake said, "Shake a leg, Pam. We've got a plane to catch. The airport limo is waiting in the driveway to take us to Logan Airport."

We encountered no construction or accident problems on the trip to East Boston, and Jake managed to squeeze in a catnap en route. While checking our luggage, Jake said, "I don't know if taking the red-eye was such a good idea. When I was in the service, it'd take me a couple of days to get over the jet lag. I never could sleep on a plane."

Right after we arrived at the gate, we filed onto the plane and were soon settled into our seats. Jake said, "I'm glad you had all those air travel mileage points accumulated. The leg room in this Virgin Atlantic's Upper Class Seating is certainly much better. It's sure different from a jump seat in a military transport. I know we could afford to pay the full fare, but my mother was a Scot, so I tend to lean toward the thrifty side."

As I squeezed his hand, I said, "I'm glad we were able to obtain seating with more space for you to stretch out, darling."

"Do you want me to inflate your neck pillow?" Jake asked.

"No, I'll be fine without it, thank you. Is there anything you need before I sack out for the duration of the flight?" I said.

"I'm all set with this Spenser novel by Robert B. Parker I've been planning to read. If you do fall asleep, how much notice would you like to have for freshening up in the morning before we land?"

"An hour or so would be fine, Jake. I'm sure there'll be a line for the lavatory any later than that. As soon as we're off the runway, I'll be able to rest my head in your lap for a while," I said.

"Pleasant dreams my love," Jake said as he blew me a kiss.

I said, "Je t'aime aussi."

Jake managed to finish reading most of the book during the course of a smooth trip with almost no turbulence, save a steady boost from a welcome tailwind. The plane started to descend after a pleasant flight, and he gave me a gentle nudge. "Pam, coffee and orange juice are here. It's 6:30 AM Heathrow time. Is there anything else you want?"

"Mmmmmm. Just you. Only you. What time did you say it is?" I asked, still only half awake.

"Past sunrise on this side of the pond or 6:30 AM, local time, but 1:30 AM real time in New England. We'll be touching down on the tarmac about 7:20 AM. The sunrise was spectacular from up here, by the way."

"Did you manage to get any sleep at all, Jake ?"

"No. I rested my eyes for a while, but I'm glad I can finally stand and get the kinks out. I was starting to get a cramp in my leg." Jake said.

"Oh, Jake, why didn't you wake me up and have me move?" I asked.

"You looked so angelic and peaceful, sweetheart. There was no reason one of us couldn't get some sleep," he said.

The plane arrived on time, but we hurried to the baggage claim; so we wouldn't be late for my appointment, only to wait for what seemed to be an eternity. Jake said, "I thought our bags would never show up. They were probably the last to come off the plane. I'm glad you know how to travel light though."

I said, "Barclays reserved a black taxicab for us to get to our meeting at their headquarters. The driver will meet and greet us just outside the entrance. It sure beats messing around with transfers on the Underground. They wanted to send a limo, but I told them that would not be necessary. It's 25 miles from Heathrow but will only take about an hour, depending on traffic. "Here he is. I'm Pamela Mullen. We'd like to go to One Churchill Place at Canary Warf please."

The airport black cab driver seemed to know all the side streets to take every time congested traffic built up in front of us. Having made the arrangements, Barclays would be billed for the ride, but I gave the man a generous tip anyway after he carried our bags into the reception lobby at the Barclays Bank headquarters.

I turned to the desk and said, "Good morning. We have an appointment with Mr. Leslie Longstaff of International Operations. We're from Grady Trading Company in the States. Here is my card."

The receptionist dialed up to Longstaff's office. Upon completion of her call, she said, "Mr. Longstaff's personal assistant will be down to get you directly. Please feel free to leave your luggage in the wardrobe on your left. May I get you anything while you wait?"

I said, "No, we're all set, but thank you for asking."

Jake had no sooner stored the bags when Mr. Longstaff's assistant showed up to lead us to the elevator and the corner office on the top floor. I entered the room first and greeted Leslie with a big hug.

I said, “Leslie, it’s such a pleasure to see you again. I checked my schedule, and I haven’t been on your side of the pond for three years. How is that possible? I love your new corporate headquarters building. If my office was on the top floor overlooking London, I don’t know how much work I could get done with this kind of view.”

Leslie advised, “The original design for the building was to have fifty stories, but after 9-11 we felt it would be far too tempting a target for terrorists, so we scaled back the plans to thirty-one floors. Once the novelty wears off, the view is only what one sees out the window, and you tend to ignore it though.”

“Leslie, this is Jacob Wells, my significant other and the love of my life. Jake, this is Leslie L. Longstaff, Barclays’ managing director of International Operations.”

“How do you do, sir? It’s a pleasure to meet you, Mr. Longstaff,” Jake said, shaking Leslie’s extended hand.

“Jake, I’m very pleased to meet you as well, but please call me Leslie. If Pamela thinks that highly of you, then you’re aces in my book. Pamela, you’re looking as ravishing as ever. You haven’t changed a bit, and your smile still lights up a room.

“You were quite cryptic in your message, so I’m not quite certain I’m fully prepared for this meeting. Perhaps you could explain in more detail what brings you all the way over here, so I can be sure you leave with all the information you require.”

I said, “We’ve been talking about taking a holiday together for the summer and thought I might resolve a sensitive issue for a client while we’re here.”

“Of course, anything for you, my dear. I’ll be pleased to offer assistance in any manner that I possibly can,” Leslie said.

"A client of Grady's Trading Company has been manufacturing electronic devices in South Korea for several years to supply their sister divisions within their corporate structure and other customers throughout Asia. Their South Korean division has been paying all the applicable taxes, fees, and necessary bribes to keep their operation going. They assured us they have complied with all the countless government restrictions there.

"As a service to sister divisions, they also have accepted and transferred orders from mutual customers. Now the Republic of Korea wants them to pay taxes and duties on goods that were manufactured outside of South Korea and shipped directly to Hong Kong and Singapore. The billing came from the manufacturing division in the States, but payments were remitted through Barclays in Singapore or Hong Kong in all cases," I said.

"I say, that is a bit of a sticky wicket, Pamela. How can I help?" Leslie asked.

"They suspect a disgruntled Korean employee in their firm saw the paperwork or perhaps an individual at Barclays noted the financial transactions and wanted a cut. Our client thinks the US operation can work directly with the customers in other parts of Asia to keep the South Korean Government out of the loop.

"Now they need a new banking system over there that can handle transactions without information leaks. GTC couldn't help them because we rely on Barclays for our transfers in Asia. I'm looking for recommendations for reliable financial trading companies in Hong Kong and Singapore without Barclays connections," I said.

"Pamela, this is not only extremely unusual, but it's somewhat of a queer request. I fully understand your concerns and rationale, however. I have made very discreet inquiries on your behalf to see what I could come up with. I believe the contents of this dossier will meet all the requirements, which you have delineated quite nicely," Leslie said.

"Leslie, thank you so very much. I recognize how very busy you must be. If I knew of any other alternatives I wouldn't have asked, but I needed input from an impeccable source that I could trust implicitly," I said.

"Yes, yes, of course, Pamela. I was more than happy to look into this matter for you. I know you would do the same for me if I needed assistance in the States. Speaking of which, how soon will you be returning stateside?" Leslie asked.

"We are booked for a return flight from Heathrow on 30 August," I replied.

Leslie said, "Please give me a call before you leave. I'd like to take you and Jake out to lunch. Perhaps we can arrange to get together with Marjorie. It isn't often we get a chance to meet one of our favorite people outside of the business day."

I said, "That would be wonderful, Leslie. I can't thank you enough for all your help. I'm sure my client will be relieved, being able to select an alternative to rid themselves of this political nightmare. Please give my best to Marjorie."

Leslie said "Unfortunately, I'm meeting with members of our government for lunch today, but I was happy to squeeze you in. Please plan on a leisurely lunch in a more relaxed setting the next time you call. Jake, it's been a real pleasure to meet you. I'm thrilled Pamela finally met someone to share her life with. She always did work too hard. Take extra special care of her. She is truly a gem."

Extending his hand, Jake replied, "She is indeed. It was very nice to meet you as well, Leslie. Thank you for the courtesies extended and your time."

Leslie said, "Think nothing of it, Jake. The pleasure is all mine. Pamela, you always have a way of brightening my day. It was wonderful seeing you again. I'll have my assistant arrange for another taxi to take you wherever you would like to go next."

We found our way down to the lobby, turned in our security badges, and retrieved our luggage.

16

As we stepped out the door of the lobby, another black cab pulled up. I said, "That must be our taxi over there."

Once we were on our way toward our hotel near Kensington Gardens, Jake appeared to be confused, so he turned to me and asked with a serious expression on his face, "Is any part of what you told Leslie true?"

"Maybe a little, but I needed a plausible explanation to get the names of money traders under the radar that might be laundering Iranian oil money to arm terrorists. He couldn't know that we are doing work for the CIA. That could put him at risk, as well," I said.

"So how will I know if you ever lie to me? You're so good at it," Jake said with a half smile that accentuated his dimples.

"It takes years and years of practice, my love," I said and kissed him on the cheek.

Jake said, "Those CIA guys are pretty good, Pam. I only spotted a couple of cars that could have been on our tail when we were on the way over here from Heathrow Airport. The taxi was probably a better choice than a limo, which would have been much easier to spot and keep track of. I assume we're on our own now."

"Except for getting this package from Leslie to our embassy tomorrow morning, our work is done here," I said. "We're ready to kick back and have fun as tourists for a change."

Jake asked, "Do you have any preference where you'd like to have a late afternoon lunch?"

"I'm totally open to suggestions, since we're now officially on holiday, as they are fond of saying over here," I said. "I've finally got you all to myself and don't have to share you with anyone. Did you have something specific in mind?"

"It just so happens; I asked the cab driver we had this morning what he could recommend for lunch when you were on the phone confirming our arrival with Leslie. He said the former head chef from Kensington Place is now at Le Café Anglais. It's reportedly one of the best French bistros in London. The kitchen is open for lunch until 3:30 PM, so we have plenty of time to get there."

"Driver, please take us to the Royal Garden Hotel to register and drop off our luggage. Then we'd like to go to Le Café Anglais," I said.

Upon arriving at the restaurant, I decided upon the special of the day. Jake simply said, "Le poulet francoi, s'il vous plait." The waiter informed him that he was filling in for a bloke across the hall in his apartment building and didn't understand what Jake said. Jake pointed to the line item on the menu and said with a deadpan expression, "I'll have the French hen please."

I managed to suppress a giggle. We both were otherwise impressed with the service and the presentation of the food in the restored building that somehow had managed to survive the German bombings during the war. The combination of the views from the picture windows and use of judicious splashes of color in the dining room made for a very pleasant atmosphere.

Following dessert, Jake asked, "Well, what did you think of the meal, Pam?"

"I can't believe I ate the whole thing. I was starving after missing breakfast and lunch. The duck salad with girolles mushrooms, followed by seared mackerel, peas, and gooseberry sauce were just divine. I probably could have done without the chocolate roulade with raspberries for dessert though.

Now I need some exercise to work it off."

"A stroll through Kensington Gardens might be just the ticket, Pam. I'm sort of stuffed myself." Jake said, patting his tummy. "It's a little over a mile from here on the other side of Hyde Park."

We were both full and somewhat sluggish getting up from the table, still coping with the effects of jet lag. Jake paid for the meal, and we walked out to Kensington Road to head for Kensington Gardens.

Crossing the street and entering the pathway through the iron gates of Kensington Gardens, Jake said, "There's the Diana Memorial Playground. According to the sign, it was designed for children to learn to use their imaginations, including those with disabilities. They even have special flowers and plants for vision-impaired kids to smell and touch.

"That looks like the Kensington Palace over on the right. I read they spent the equivalent of 18 million in US dollars renovating it before Kate and William could move in. If you don't mind, I'd like to walk through the Gardens to see the history of science and medicine museum on the other side. According to the map I picked up at the airport, it's across Kensington Gore on Exhibition Road behind Royal Albert Hall."

"No problem. I'd be interested in seeing that myself. Look at Round Pond with all the birds over there. Those pigeons are twice the size of ours back home. The ducks, geese, and swans all seem to get along well. What do you suppose that swan is doing near the edge?" I asked.

"It seems to be bobbing for that tennis ball, but he drops it to the bottom as soon as he picks it out of the water with his bill. Then he does it all over again. Maybe he's in training to be a ball swan at Wimbledon."

I laughed out loud when I formed a mental image of a swan flying around center court chasing tennis balls. Hopefully, he wouldn't be squawking "Aflac" with the annoying noise in the television commercials back home.

Jake said, "That wasn't that funny." When I explained why I was laughing, Jake then chuckled too.

When we got a little further down the path, Jake looked up ahead of us and said, "Wow! At 175 feet tall, the Albert Memorial statue looks huge, even from here. This brochure says it illustrates the span of the British Empire stretching to the four continents and depicts commerce, engineering, manufacturing, and agriculture."

"The sculpture is exquisite, but I need to cross the street to see if Prince Albert's Hall has a ladies' loo before I create a puddle."

Jake seemed to be amazed that I could cross the road that fast and almost had trouble keeping up with me. He waited outside until I finally reappeared at the door.

Jake said, "From the serene look on your face, I take it you are finally relieved."

"That was a close call. I almost met my Waterloo. Perhaps I had a little too much wine with lunch. Are you ready to see the museum now? Every time I've been in London on business, I never had a chance to see any of the sights," I said.

"Same here when I was in the service. I'd like to see the advances in transportation, medicine, and manufacturing displays. I've heard they're really impressive. There's the main entrance over there on the right," Jake said.

As we entered the energy hall at the ground floor level, Jake dragged his feet looking at each exhibit and he read all the plaques because he obviously didn't want to miss anything. I didn't mind since he was in his element and appeared to be enjoying himself immensely. Next he wanted to stop at the space exploration display down the hall.

Jake asked about and was informed that the Apollo 10 Command Module that went on the moon mission immediately prior to the first lunar landing was next to the science museum gallery up on the first floor. Jake commented that he would have expected to find it located in their space gallery.

Up the next flight of stairs as we approached the Apollo Command Module, I said, "Jake, I may be imagining things, but that looks like the couple I saw in the energy hall at ground level. Now that I think about it, he reminds me of the guy that was staring at us on the old train in the Berkshire Mountains."

"You might be right, Pam. It could be a coincidence, but why don't we go up to see the medical science exhibits on the fifth floor and work our way down?" Jake suggested.

"Okay, but why would anyone be following us? I asked.

"I don't know. I've kept such a low profile I don't think it could be anything to do with the work I've been doing at the Quabbin Reservoir," Jake said.

Once we got off the elevator on the fifth floor, I felt relieved and decided it may have been a fluke that the other couple just had an interest in the same exhibits. Jake said he thought perhaps one or both might have been scientists. That was until he spotted the pair emerging from the elevator. "We need to go outside and find a red Telcom phone box right away."

"Why? Are you going to change into your Superman outfit?"

"No. I need to call Walter Pickering of British Secret Intelligence Service at Vauxhall Cross here in London. I worked with him when he was in the Special Reconnaissance Regiment in Afghanistan at the same time I was there when I served in the army. I don't know who we can trust over here, and we can't take a chance that our cell phones are being monitored. Make sure your phone is turned off and stays that way," Jake cautioned.

We ran through a door marked "stairs" taking two steps at a time until we reach the ground floor and hurried out the exit. Walking at a brisk pace down the street, we encountered a bank of a half dozen red phone booths. Jake entered a red box that looked like an old fashioned pay phone booth from the States and dialed a number on a slip of paper from his wallet.

I wondered to myself why so many of the red boxes were clustered together and how the Brits got along with so few cell phones compared to the people in the States.

As Jake exited the phone box, the man from the museum appeared, seemingly out of nowhere. Pulling a knife, he lunged forward; but Jake grabbed his wrist with both hands, sidestepped, and used the attacker's momentum to slam him headfirst into the adjacent brick wall. He slowly crumpled into a pile on the pavement. Jake kicked the knife away while removing his necktie to bind the man's hands behind him before he came to.

I tried to recover from my shock due to what just happened as Jake took off his belt and handed it to me. "Tie his feet with this while I watch in case his partner shows up," Jake told me.

"Jake! Are you okay? How did you do that?" I asked.

"I'm fine. I may have nerve damage in my spine, but my muscles still work. I'll probably be sore for a few days though.

Didn't I mention I was in Special Forces in the army?"

"What are Special Forces?"

"You probably know them as the Green Berets. I was in a gorilla combat and reconnaissance team in Afghanistan. That's part of the reason I was selected for the Quabbin Task Force in case unfriendlies were encountered," Jake said.

"You didn't have a costume on when you emerged from the phone booth. Do you at least have a big *S* printed on your chest that I haven't seen? Sorry, I'm so keyed up I don't know what I'm saying. I'm only trying to relieve nervous tension.

Were you able to reach your friend Walter?"

"He said he's not that far away, and he'll be here shortly. Speak of the devil, that looks like him pulling up now. Walter, you old dog, how have you been?" Jake asked with a big grin on his face.

"Jake! It looks like you've been up to your old tricks again. Who is the bloke you have got hog tied on the bloody pavement, and more important, who is this gorgeous vision you have at your side?" Walter said.

"Walter, this is Pamela. I don't know what I've done to deserve her, but she has changed my whole perspective on life. As far as the creep wearing my tie and belt is concerned, your guess is as good as mine. I've been watching for his female partner, so I haven't had a chance to check him for identification yet." Jake said.

"Well, Jake, after I get more reliable restraints on him, we'll put him in the back of the van before anyone sees him. Then we won't need to explain him to the local police. We can do his processing after we get him to MI6 at Vauxhall Cross to find out who he is and what he was up to." Walter said.

Walter grabbed the attacker under the arms, and Jake took his feet as they unceremoniously deposited the dead weight behind the rear seat of the van. The attacker was still out cold, but Walter fastened a gag over his mouth anyway. Jake got in the back seat, so he could keep an eye on the prisoner, and Walter slammed the door shut. I rode at the shotgun position in the front seat.

As Walter pulled away from the curb, he asked, "Do you want to tell me more about what kind of trouble you have got yourself into this time mate?"

Jake responded, "We have no idea. I'd been working undercover on protecting the mainland of the United States from potential terrorist attacks without incident when I informed our government of my new relationship with Pamela. After checking her background, she was asked if she could help them out in an advisory capacity because of her extensive experience in international finance. We thought we could help dig up some information for the CIA while we were over here on holiday for the summer."

Walter asked, "Who knew you were coming here and what you would be doing?"

Jake said, "Nobody that we know of other than our respective government agents in the states and a business acquaintance of Pamela's at Barclays Bank's main office on Canary Warf here in London. That would include his staff that made the arrangements for our visit earlier today. We assumed there must be a leak, so we didn't dare make contact with anyone on our cell phones. We also shut our cells off, so our movements couldn't be tracked. Because no problems were anticipated, we didn't prearrange emergency contingencies or find out who else we could trust over here. That's why I rang you up."

"You'll have to excuse me for a few more moments whilst I concentrate on my driving since the traffic is picking up more than a few beats. Did I mention that the drivers here in London are absolute idiots?" Walter commented as he focused his attention on the road ahead.

Jake said, "That's what I thought too, Walter, but I wasn't going to say anything about it. There's no sense in upsetting the natives. Who knows how belligerent they might become? This guy in the back came at me with a knife, and I wasn't even driving."

Walter said, "If that's your story mate, you'd better stick with it. Not that any sane or rational individual would believe it, of course."

Just then an old Mercedes came screaming out of a side street, hot on our tail. Shots rang out. As he stomped on the accelerator, Walter said, "This agency van is supposedly bulletproof, but just in case, you two might want to slouch down in your seats a bit. Quick, Pamela, punch star 5 on the radio console if you would."

Walter began zigging and zagging through multiple lanes of traffic as a static filled voice came over the speaker, "Dispatch. Please identify yourself and state the nature of your emergency."

"This is Colonel Water Pickering of MI6 in van 23, requesting assistance. Shots fired. Headed east on Knightsbridge at Sloane Street. We are being pursued by a vintage black Mercedes sedan in heavy traffic. Executing evasive maneuvers. Will turn north on New Park Lane at Wellington Arch then proceed west on Bayswater Road."

"Roger that," boomed the disembodied voice. "We have your location on the screen. Units dispatched to intercept."

Walter passed his gun back to Jake and said, "Here, use this if they manage to pull up alongside."

Jake rolled down the rear window and leaned out enough to shoot out one of the front tires of the Mercedes. The car swerved as sparks flew off the rim of the deflated tire. Turning at the Marble Arch, two silver BMW patrol cars came up behind the Mercedes with blue lights flashing and sirens wailing their Be-Bop song from Oxford Street, but the black sedan immediately turned north on Edgeware Road with the London Police in hot pursuit.

We couldn't be certain, but it sounded like the Mercedes crashed as it turned the corner.

As if nothing out of the ordinary had happened, Walter turned to me and asked, "How are you holding up, Pamela?"

"I'm, I'm fine, I think," I said, barely able to get the words out.

"How about you, Jake? Is the prisoner awake yet?" Walter inquired.

"I think he must be bored. He slept through the whole thing," Jake said as casually as he would when talking about the weather.

I didn't realize how much I was still shaking when I asked, "How, how did you two get accustomed to this sort of thing without getting stressed out?"

"It didn't come easy, but right now you need to relax. You're as white as a sheet. Take deep breaths, but inhale and exhale slowly," Jake said.

With that, Walter continued to loop around Kensington Gardens and Hyde Park to resume our original route. "Drat it all, I suppose this will mean I'll have to fill out another stack of paperwork for the London Police, won't I?" Walter said to no one in particular.

"Here's MI6 headquarters at Vauxhall coming up now. One would think that the Secret Intelligence Service headquarters for the United Kingdom would be hidden, but there it is for all to see. That's our Foreign Military Intelligence for you."

Colonel Pickering drove up to the gate, presented his identification to the guard on duty, and then pulled through as soon as the motorized black iron gate was fully opened. Once inside, Walter had us sign in the register to receive visitor badges. He then instructed the sergeant on the desk to have the prisoner in the back of the van tended to and brought upstairs to detention for questioning. Walter led us to the elevator and escorted us from there into a huge conference room.

Once seated, I had the impression we were being watched by a rogue's gallery with the walls covered with darkened oil paintings of the Royal Family and their ancestors in gilded frames. Even with subtle movements in our chairs, the eyes in the paintings still appeared to be focused on us. The remainder of the wall space was occupied with pictures of the former British Empire, maps, and pull down screens. I was surprised there were no windows. I assumed it was for security purposes. "What can I get for you? Coffee, tea, Coke?" Walter asked.

Jake said, "We ate a big meal at Le Café Anglais this afternoon, so we're still full, but thank you anyway, Walter."

Jake and I proceeded to describe the events of the day and where we had been in our travels around the city of London without divulging the purpose of our mission. Walter then pushed a red button on the side of the phone.

A man in military uniform showed up at the door. Walter beckoned him in with a flick of his fingers and introduced him to us as Lieutenant Peter West. "Peter, this is Pamela Mullen and Jacob Wells, representing the Central Intelligence Agency in the States. Please join us and take notes of what needs to be done. There has been a security breach, and the ramifications are not yet fully understood. No one is to be informed of any details they do not need to know to carry out their assignments." Walter stated with a very stern look.

"Yes, sir, understood," replied Peter.

Walter continued, "The CIA headquarters in Langley, Virginia is five hours behind us. The first thing that needs to be done is to contact the CIA agents Taylor Young and Manny Rodriquez on a coded scrambler. Advise them to get back to me through the usual secure channels to discuss a leak of classified information, possibly within their organization.

"Next, arrange for a meeting for us first thing in the morning with Mr. Matthew Lynch, the US ambassador at the American Embassy in Grosvenor Square.

"Third, locate the managing director of International Operations at Barclays Bank on Canary Warf. His name is Leslie L. Longstaff. Explain that we have reason to believe there might possibly be an electronic bug or wiretap in his office, and we'll send someone over to check it out. Tell him we don't think he's in any danger, but we'd like to provide a security detail to follow him for a few days to make certain.

"Last, obtain this couple's luggage from the Royal Garden Hotel at Kensington High Street and bring it here, following the standard security precautions. That should do it for now, Peter. Thank you."

Walter left for a few moments to advise the people up his chain of command about what was transpiring and then returned to the conference room.

He made a quick call to arrange to get us to a safe house with extra security on the outskirts of London. Following a second call, he turned to us and said, "They've identified your attacker through Interpol as a Saudi radical, but so far he's not talking. The people in the black Mercedes abandoned the vehicle when it crashed and fled on foot. Apparently, they got away. The car had been reported as stolen.

Your CIA contacts are en route and will arrive at Heathrow early tomorrow morning. Since I'm already involved, our governments have authorized you to provide complete disclosure for us to work together on this matter."

Jake said, "It's great to see you again and all that, Walter, but I'm sorry if I am making your life a bit more complicated."

"Nonsense, my boy, it's all in a day's work. That's what I'm here for. We're still on the same side after all. Now that you are officially allowed to explain the details, what else can you tell me about the purpose of your mission here in London?" Walter inquired.

I first looked over to Jake for a nod of acknowledgement then back to Walter. "Actually, it's my mission for the CIA. The National Security Administration (NSA) hasn't been able to follow the money trails from the Iranian oil blockade through Asian financial institutions to fund terrorist plots since Iran pulled their money out of the Cayman Islands, Switzerland, and London. The United Nations' embargo on Iran has more holes than a sieve, but the CIA couldn't identify where they switched their oil money laundering operations to in Asia.

"The NSA feels the terrorist plots can be identified and prevented if they know when and where large sums of money are being deployed to finance them. I came here to enlist the aid of one of my closest business associates without revealing the true purpose of my visit. As previously mentioned, he is Leslie L. Longstaff, a managing director of Barclays Bank who gave me a complete dossier today with new information on Singapore and Hong Kong that I have not yet had a chance to review."

Walter said, "Perhaps your friend rang the wrong bell when doing his research on your behalf and tipped them off that they were being investigated. Then again, it is possible his inquiry came at a time when the Muslim extremists were launching another major offensive to make a political point. The answer to which Asian trading companies the CIA is looking for might be found in the recommendations contained in the dossier, but that's for someone above my pay grade to determine. The scan on Longstaff's office for bugs and wiretaps should be completed shortly to see if that could have struck the chord that caused you to come under surveillance."

Jake said, "That might be true, but perhaps we were being followed long before that. I don't think my undercover work as a wildlife photographer and fisherman would have raised any suspicions. We have no way of knowing, but I just recalled that my task force at the Quabbin Reservoir rounded up a group of seven Muslim chemical engineers who were trespassing after dark. We turned them over to the Massachusetts State Police, but they were subsequently released. They might have been able to get my name from the arrest report I had to fill out.

"Based on routine analyses of greater Boston's water supply, trace amounts of various toxins would mysteriously show up periodically. We suspected these were from tests being conducted to ascertain source to end user concentration ratios and flow times from the reservoir. I was assigned to assemble a task force to resolve the issue.

"There were CIA agents watching our backs from the airport here to London's financial district, but they were supposed to leave us on our own once that meeting was completed. From that point, we were going on holiday once the dossier was delivered to the US Embassy tomorrow."

Walter leaned back in his plush swivel conference chair and stroked his chin. "Unless these CIA agents from the States can offer additional insights tomorrow, we don't have much to go on, do we?"

Just then, Lieutenant West appeared in the window of the door to the conference room, and Walter signaled for him to enter. "Yes, Peter, what is it?"

Peter said, "The luggage has been retrieved from the Royal Garden Hotel and scanned. There is no evidence of having been tampered with, and they are devoid of tracking devices. The meeting at the US Embassy has been set up and confirmed by all attendees for nine tomorrow morning."

Walter said, "Excellent. Thank you, Peter. Please inform them at the contingency desk that we're ready for transportation to the London safe house with the usual escort provisions. We will be down in the lift to meet them at the garage level presently."

Walter turned to us and said, "Unless you can think of any pertinent details, I should be aware of or have any questions, perhaps we should be off. I know you've had an extremely long day after your overnight flight."

Following a moment of reflection, Jake said, "None that come to mind. I must say though; it does feel great to be working with you once again Walter. Just like old times."

Walter replied, "I hope not Jake. I really hope not. Those were very dangerous situations we went through together back then, weren't they?"

Walter suggested that the documents from Barclays on the Asian trading companies be photocopied for storage at MI6 for safe keeping in case they were what the Saudi was after. He said, "Perhaps we hit the jackpot so we can trace the money paths and uncover the major terrorists' plots."

I noted that I should keep the Barclays originals to turn over to the CIA at the American Embassy after review in case I need to discuss the report with Leslie or Taylor at some future date. That being accomplished, Peter backed up an enclosed panel van with tinted windows to the elevator door in the garage, so we could enter directly without being seen.

17

In the process of being driven to a fortified safe house, I only had a New York minute to gather my thoughts as we wove through the evening traffic. I was at once elated to be sharing this adventure of a lifetime with Jake and chagrinned at the same time to realize that our very lives could be in danger of being snuffed out without a moment's notice. Just how safe could a safe house in the middle of England be? I will have to depend upon Jake and his friend Walter Pickering to look after my safety...and Jake's.

Certain areas of New York City are extremely dangerous and to be avoided, but I was always comfortable in the neighborhoods of my Wall Street office and my apartment building. Unfortunately, here was a situation where I could only rely on the choices of others. To preserve my sanity, I'd have to trust Jake's judgment and try to remain calm.

The van pulled into a garage attached to a nondescript, two-story, brick-faced house on the outskirts of London. It resembled all the others on the street, which were rebuilt after the whole area was leveled by German bombs in World War II. The garage door was closed before Walter and Peter climbed out of the van with guns drawn. A code was entered into the touch keypad next to the inside door and the latch clicked open. They carefully went into the house through the kitchen door ahead of Jake and me. After they determined the MI6 security team had everything under control, they signaled for us to follow them inside.

In the kitchen, a veritable feast fit for a king was laid out on the table. Peter reached for a croissant roll only to have his hand slapped by Harry, a gruff-looking sergeant. In a raspy voice, he growled, "Those are for our guests."

Walter said, "Pay him no mind; he's a teddy bear on the inside and a graduate of Le Cordon Bleu cooking school in Paris. Just don't put an automatic rifle in his hands. He develops a severely mean streak in combat situations. I hope you two have worked up an appetite. Harry hates to see people leave a table of his hungry."

Jake looked at Walter and asked, "Are you not going to join us? We can regale Pamela with our Afghanistan exploits."

Walter shook his head and said, "'Fraid not, Jake me lad. Peter and I only have a short time remaining before your folks at Langley close up shop for the night. We must be sure their team is on its way here, and all the staff at the American Embassy in London is ready to convene with the rest of us first thing in the morning.

"Pamela, it's been a delight to meet Jake's new partner in life. He's one lucky man from what I've seen. Please take care of my boy here. He needs a lot of looking after to keep his nose clean and to stay out of trouble."

"Don't worry, Walter, you can count on me to follow up on that," I answered with a smile.

Jake patted him on the shoulder while shaking his hand. "Thank you for everything, Walter. I knew I could always depend on you to come through in a pinch."

Walter turned and said, "One last thing, Pamela, the security systems employed here use the latest technology available. Our lads are the very best, so not to worry, you'll be well protected. If you're not aware of it, Jake is no slouch himself in that department."

I gave him a big hug. "Thank you for taking care of everything, Walter. I feel safe with Jake around, but I feel even better knowing you've got his back. It was a pleasure meeting you too. We'll see you in the morning."

Peter and Walter left to return to MI6 to complete the arrangements for the next day. As the car drove off, Harry said, "I sure hope you Yanks are hungry."

Jake turned to look at the table covered with an array of candied yams, seafood bisque, quiche Lorraine, chateaubriand, coquilles St. Jacques with wild rice and mushrooms, shrimp sauce-coated cauliflower, and a Black Forest cake. He said to Harry, "The table is only set for two. Won't you and the rest of your team be joining us for dinner?"

Harry responded, "We ate before you came to be sure we'd be ready in case there was any kind of trouble."

Jake said, "Harry, there's enough food on the table for five or six more people."

Harry answered, "That may be true enough. I'm not used to cooking for less than a squad in the military. It's hard to scale the recipes down in my large pots and pans. No problem, I'll put anything left over in the refrigerator. Now if you'll excuse me, I have to man my post. Enjoy."

Jake said, "Everything looks and smells delicious. You didn't have to go through all this trouble, but thank you very much, Harry."

Harry said, "I enjoy cooking, but I like to see people happy to have a good meal at the end of the day even more. When you're finished eating, you'll find your luggage in the room with a telly at the top of the stairs to the right.

"Make sure you keep the blinds drawn and stay away from the windows. Only use the lights on the same side of the room with the windows so as not to cast a shadow. We'll wake you early enough in the morning to get to the embassy on time for your meeting. Good night and pleasant dreams."

Jake and I simultaneously said, "Good night, Harry," so it sounded like it was rehearsed. Harry did a little double take and exited through the doorway with a wink and a thumbs up.

Jake and I dug into a scrumptious meal after a very trying day, savoring each morsel. Jake commented, "If Harry was the cook in my outfit, I might have been tempted to reenlist if I didn't still have the bullet fragments in my spine."

When we finished eating, we put our dishes in the sink and climbed the stairs to our room. I told Jake, "I have to go through the package from Barclays Bank just so I know what's in there for tomorrow's discussion. Why don't you see if you can find BBC News on the TV?"

Jake asked, "Is there anything I can get for you or do to help?"

"No, thank you. This won't take long. I should finish up reviewing the dossier in twenty or thirty minutes. You must be exhausted after not sleeping on the plane," I said as I went over to give him a long, lingering, passionate kiss. "You go get ready for bed, and I'll join you shortly."

Jake opened the luggage and changed. After he found the BBC channel, he turned down the bed and slipped under the covers. I curled up in club chair in the corner to look at the paperwork Leslie had prepared. I was surprised it took over an hour to finish reading all the enclosed material since the financial status and backgrounds on each of the candidate Asian trading companies were so completely detailed. Then again, because Leslie was always so thorough, I couldn't imagine him putting forth anything less than his very best effort.

I turned to find my mate sound asleep, so I leaned over to kiss his forehead and quietly whispered, "Poor baby, you have to be so tired." Then I turned off the TV and light, slid under the covers, and snuggled up next to him wondering how I managed to get along without him all those years.

We are awakened by a gentle tapping from the hallway. I slipped on my robe and opened the door to see Harry standing there. He said, "Good morning. Breakfast will be ready in a half hour."

"Thank you, Harry. We'll be down shortly," I said.

The sun was streaming in on both sides of the blinds. Jake was still trying to open both eyes at the same time but was somewhat disoriented. "Where are we? No, never mind. I remember now. Good morning, gorgeous. You look beautiful this morning as always."

"Thank you, love, but if you were fully awake, you'd be able to see I haven't even put on my face yet," I said.

"Did I ever tell you how pretty you are with a naked face?" Jake asked.

"Yes, you have. Too many times to count, but you know it's not true," I said.

"Pam, even when we're old, gray and wrinkled, you'll still be the most attractive woman on the planet to me," Jake answered.

"Jake, flattery will get you everywhere with me, but you have to get up and get cracking because we probably will have another fast-paced day ahead of us," I said, thinking about all that had transpired yesterday. Perhaps it won't be so bad once the dangerous elements are under control.

Being short on time, we competed for shower, sink and mirror space; by alternating positions. Quickly we repacked our luggage and Jake carried it down the stairs to breakfast. As we walked into the kitchen Jake said, "Good morning Harry. The omelets and the coffee smell absolutely great."

"Thank you. You probably will be in for another busy day. There's no telling when you'll see your next meal, so eat up and you can be on your way. Colonel Pickering and Lieutenant West should be here shortly to pick you up," Harry said.

Like the dinner Harry had prepared for the night before, the light, fluffy omelets were fantastic. Just as we finished eating, we heard the garage door opening. Walter stuck his head in the kitchen and asked if we were ready to go as Peter closed the garage door.

"All set." Jake said, as he turned to Harry to shake his hand. "Thanks for all the hospitality and protection."

I said, "Thank you again, Harry, everything was delicious."

As Jake grabbed the luggage, I started to follow him out to the van when Harry said, "It was nice meeting you two, but I hope you don't need a safe house the next time you're in London. Good-bye and good luck."

Once we were hidden from external view within the van, the garage door was opened, and we took off for the embassy. Peter drove carefully so as not to attract undue attention or get pulled over for speeding. Walter turned from the front passenger seat and inquired, "Were the accommodations in the safe house satisfactory last night?"

I replied, "Jake was so tired that he probably didn't notice, but everything was super, especially the food. Harry outdid himself on both meals. Thank you for asking.

"I also wanted you and Peter to know that we really appreciate you helping us out of the predicament we're in. I'm new to this shady side of the justice stuff and didn't know where we could turn to for help. We were fortunate that Jake knew how to get in touch with you."

Walter responded, "If you two can venture across the pond, lending a helping hand is the least we can do as good hosts. We have the same objectives, and whatever we can do to make America a safer place will accomplish the same thing here in the United Kingdom."

Peter pulled up to the embassy gate and presented his credentials. The officer on duty verified we were expected by the ambassador and flipped the switch for the motorized, chain-driven cast iron gate. As instructed, Peter followed the yellow line on the tarmac around the back of the building complex and into the underground parking area where we disembarked.

One of the guards inside escorted us to the third floor conference room where we met Manny and Taylor of the CIA; Sir James Cooper, director of the British Secret Intelligence Service known as MI6; John Campbell, the Canadian high commissioner; Theodore Wisniewski, the US ambassador; and too many others to remember. Everyone took their piping hot mugs of coffee or tea with pastries to their seats at the long, polished dark walnut conference table, and there was a round of introductions.

As the senior officer on the case for MI6, Colonel Pickering offered a brief synopsis of what happened and why so far. He informed the assembled group; MI6 had just learned from Interpol that the prints of the Saudi who attacked Jacob Wells belong to Abdul Al Yami who was last known to be in Yemen.

An immediate din arose after everyone speculated about what that meant, posed questions, and talked simultaneously. Pickering bellowed, "Gentlemen!" as if he were an army drill sergeant, followed by a subdued "And ladies," to attain some semblance of order and decorum. He continued, "I have just explained essentially all we know at this point in time. We are gathered here to inform you of the current status, which has been completed. Secondly, we need to determine the course of action required to quell or minimize the threat of any plots being formulated against us collectively.

"Let me reiterate, so we're all on the same page. Unless the CIA has a mole in their organization, we believe the Muslim extremists may have been inadvertently tipped off because of our inquiries into Iranian oil money funding of terrorist activities through Asia. We suspect they feel their money laundering practices, plus their trading company partners in Hong Kong and Singapore might be coming under scrutiny, thereby endangering another major plan to raise havoc somewhere else in the world. Recently obtained documents detailing potential Asian participants in the terrorists' money trails have been turned over to the CIA. A copy has been safely stored at MI6 for use within our own intelligence community.

"Outside of the people in this room, only certain authorized individuals, will be made aware of the existence of these files. Access to the information contained therein will be restricted to a select few, on an as needed basis, to minimize the potential threat to the sources of the information.

"We have arranged to have the CIA advisors Mullen and Wells secretly transported to Ontario by the Royal Canadian Air Force to keep a low profile until everything is sorted out. While in Canada, Ms. Mullen will be available to assist and direct our forensic financial analysts who are following the money transfers. This will be prearranged with a limited number of specific designates in the CIA and the Canadian government. The list of these individuals will be resolved here today.

"Because Toronto is the financial capital of Canada, Pamela Mullen will use her business connections there to acquire additional information and keep track of world trends and techniques regarding international movements of large sums of money.

It goes without saying that MI6 and the CIA will be cooperating to the fullest extent possible to detect and deter any signs of Muslim extremists' aggression. We fully appreciate the assistance of the Canadians in this effort.

Unless anyone has any questions of the American advisors at this point, they will be on their way to Canada from the Royal Air Force's Northolt field in London. The CIA will remain here this morning to work out assignment details with MI6 to avoid duplication of efforts.

Since there doesn't seem to be any questions addressed to Mullen and Wells forthcoming at the moment, we wish them Godspeed and a safe journey."

18

Jake and I were escorted to the parking area and saw Peter West was once again driving the enclosed van. Upon reaching the Northolt Royal Air Force Base, we found our arrival had apparently been anticipated. After presenting his credentials, Peter was told to follow the jeep that one of the two airmen from the guard shack was starting up. We were astonished to be led directly to a pair of Canadian RCAF McDonnell Douglas CF-18 Hornet fighter jets on the tarmac that were fueled and readied for takeoff. We were told that the planes were previously scheduled to return to CFB Borden Airbase in Ontario, Canada. They explained the trip at supersonic speeds would take less than half the normal eight hours flight time that a wide body passenger aircraft would involve.

Unfortunately, due to cockpit space constraints, Jake and I would be required to fly in separate planes. This was the first time we would be apart since our journey began. The fighter jets appeared fast and powerful, but they were so tiny compared to the commercial planes I was accustomed to taking in my travels for business. As I thought about it, I started to become more than a little nervous. While I was certain the Canadians would have their top mechanics performing the maintenance and repairs on the planes, they appeared to have seen more than a fair amount of service. When I asked how old they were, I was informed planes of this reiteration were all in the range of twenty to thirty years old.

I began to wonder if there was a severe mechanical problem, could I survive a parachute ejection over the Atlantic? Worse yet, what would I do if anything happened to Jake?

Could I or would I want to go on without him? In an extremely short, albeit wonderful time span, he had become my raison d'être.

"Get a grip on yourself, Pam." I told myself. "Everything will go off fine without a hitch. These pilots wouldn't consider flying them if they weren't absolutely sure they were safe. Don't let Jake watch you become a wimp and fall apart on him. We both knew I had always managed to maintain a stronger resolve than that."

After introductions to and instructions from the pilots, we returned to the van to don our high altitude flight suits. Then we reluctantly bade farewell to Lieutenant West and thanked him once again for all his help on our behalf.

Our luggage was stowed on board the fighters, and we were assisted up the wings into the cockpits of our respective planes. Following attachment of restraint harnesses, headphones, and facemask, I received stern warnings that I was not to touch any knobs, levers, switches, bells, or whistles under any circumstances.

From the preflight briefing, I knew the takeoff in the fighter jets would be significantly faster and had a steeper rate of climb than commercial flights, but the ride would be smooth once the full cruise altitude of 36,000 feet was attained.

Although I had been cautioned that I would be subjected to twice the force of gravity during the ascent phase, I was not fully prepared for the experience. Initially, it seemed like I was being pushed back into the seat as if I were on a high speed roller coaster ride; but with the extended duration, the force on my 140 pounds of body weight doubled to 280 pounds as I was pinned to my seat. I felt fortunate that the load was distributed over my five foot ten inch tall frame.

With the blood circulation to my brain reduced, I began to feel lightheaded, and my vision faded from the full spectrum of color to shades of black and white.

After we leveled off at altitude, I started to recover and the effects diminished as I became aware of the pilot's voice in my headphones. When he repeated, "Are you doing okay?" I realized what he was saying and was able to respond, but it sounded like he was speaking to me from the inside of a giant seashell next to my ear.

As I peered through the small canopy, I realized we were over the ocean already, plowing through wispy cirrus clouds. Looking down below at the towering mountains of snow white cumulus clouds, I wished I was wearing a pair of skis to zip down them so I could bounce from one fluffy cloud to another. When my focus returned to the horizon, I noticed Jake's plane and waved. Jake or his pilot must have seen me because the other plane rocked back and forth to signal acknowledgement with the wings.

Amazed at the incredible view at this altitude and lost in my thoughts, my pilot announced on the intercom that we were passing Iceland already. Before I realized, we were descending into Toronto airspace. As we touched down on the runway, I felt relief set in as the tension in my body started to drain. Maybe I was considerably more anxious than I realized.

I was stunned to not only arrive in Canada three and a half hours after our London departure but with our luggage available and no customs agents to deal with. I noted mentally I had taken the Concord SST between Paris and New York a few times, but there wasn't that much time gain after I waited for luggage and in the line to clear customs afterward. Subsequent to a long taxi down the narrow strip of asphalt, both planes pulled into a hanger followed by an enclosed black SUV with darkened windows that apparently had been waiting for our arrival.

The hanger doors closed as soon as the turbine engines shut down. After Jake and I were helped down from the cockpits, my legs felt like rubber for a few minutes. The SUV pulled up next to the planes and a Canadian army officer hopped out of the passenger side. Jake studied the man's gait as he approached before recognition set in. "Gord! I don't believe it. What the heck are you doing here?"

The officer ran the last few steps and gave him a big hug. "Jake, you crazy son of a gun, how have you been and why are you here?"

"Excuse me, Pam, I'd like to introduce Captain Gordon; oops, now I see he's Major Gordon McNulty of the Canadian Special Operations Regiment. We served together in Afghanistan. Gord, this is the love of my life, Pamela Mullen of the Grady Trading Company in New York City." The major said, "It's a pleasure to meet you, Ms. Mullen. I'm here to protect a couple of Americans flying over here from England on a rush, hush-hush basis. That couldn't be the two of you by any chance?"

"That would be us. It's nice to meet you, major. Please call me Pam. Your pal Jake seems to know everyone in the military everywhere," I said.

"I'm sure it's just happenstance. All my friends call me Gord, I hope you will do the same, Pam. After what Jake and I have been through together, I'm surprised anyone could possibly think that Jake would need protection from anything."

I responded, "You may be right there. I've already seen him in action, even without his Superman cape."

While Jake and Gord talked, I noticed our luggage had appeared behind us. It was then I saw the pilots were almost up to the small door in the back of the hanger. I said, "They must have retrieved our bags, but we didn't get a chance to thank them for the ride."

The major said, "They were just doing their job. You were hitching a lift on the trip they were planning to get back home after their tours of duty were up anyway, so no thanks are necessary. Besides that, they were anxious to get home to their families after being away for such a long time.

"We're here to keep you out of sight and provide protection for you, so please get in the back seat. I'll put your luggage in the rear. We'll take care of returning your flight suits later."

The hanger door started its assent as soon as the major was seated in the SUV. Gord said, "The driver is Sergeant Gerald Choquette. A few people call him Jerry, but to us, he's affectionately known as Frenchy. Frenchy, say hello to

Brenda and Cliff MacOmber."

"Bonjour."

Jake wondered who selected those undercover names as he asked, "Comment alley-vous?

Frenchy replied, "Je vais bien, merci." Then he showed his identification to the security officer when he pulled up to the guard shack and was waved through the open gate in the chain link fence. He looked at Jake in the rear-view mirror and said with a big grin, "You picked up a little bit of French in Paris, yes? Their pronunciation in France gives me a headache trying to understand them."

To which Jake responded, "Over there they say the same thing about how you Canadians speak French."

Jake turned to Gord and asked, "Where are we off to now?"

"A little bed and breakfast called the Maple Leaf Inn located in the northernmost village in the city of Vaughn called Hope."

Jake said, "It's nice to know there's always hope, and it still springs eternal. Do we know what we'll be doing there?"

To which Gord replied, "I'll be darned if I know. I just found out you were coming a few hours ago. I was told not to ask any questions, but it sure is good to see you again, '*Cliff*.'"

Jake leaned toward me and whispered, "Is Pam going to find out I'm cheating on her with Brenda?

I grinned and replied, "You're not, Cliff is with Brenda."

"In that case, it looks like I dodged a bullet. I should have learned how to do that before I went to Afghanistan. Does that mean Cliff is in trouble?"

"I have no idea but dealing with Brenda is Cliff's problem."

Gord interrupted our whispering back and forth with, "Since we don't know how long you two will be here, we can arrange to get whatever you need for the long haul. I was informed that your passports and driver's licenses were lost, so we'll get you replacements, eh?"

"That would be appreciated, Gord. We'll have to come up with a list of what we think we'll need during our stay here."

At that point, Jake and I resumed our whispering. Jake told me that if we are to leave to meet people away from the inn we would need to fit in with our new identities. He said he could grow a beard and wear a baseball cap before we have our pictures taken for our photo IDs. He would have preferred a cap with a New England Patriots' logo, but he'd settle for one from the Toronto Blue Jays so as to not call attention to himself. I said I could dye my hair a different color and trim it myself. Jake cringed when I suggested we should get wedding rings if we were to pass ourselves off as a couple, but I assumed he was just clowning around being Jake or Cliff in this case.

We pulled off the main highway to a smaller paved road, which passed through open fields with cows, sheep, and crops on both sides. The distance between houses increased the further we traveled, until Frenchy turned onto a long gravel driveway that wound its way into the woods. The words "Maple Leaf Inn" could barely be made out on a faded sign with peeling paint, suspended by a pair of rusty chains.

Frenchy slowed down more as potholes were encountered with greater frequency, rocking the SUV back and forth while raising a huge cloud of dust behind us. In the distance on top of a small hill, we could see what looked like an overgrown Swiss chalet with multiple additions that could have used a fresh coat of paint. Frenchy pulled through the open doorway of the attached garage next to the house, hopped out, closed the garage door, and then opened the car door for me.

Jake was surprised that Frenchy's height was something south of five foot nothing, but his muscular build lent the impression his broad shoulders were as wide as he was tall. Frenchy hefted our bags as if they were empty and said he'd bring then up to our room.

When he disappeared from sight, Gord said to Jake, "I saw you take note of his lack of stature. One of his brothers is a jockey, but don't let his appearance fool you. If you're in a shootout or fist fight, he's the kind of guy you want to back you up. I've seen a couple of wise guys twice his size pick a fight with him in a bar. They wouldn't let him leave, so he put them both down and walked out over them."

Jake said, "Good to know."

We followed Gord through the door leading to the living room, which had a cathedral ceiling. There also was a balcony surrounding the room at the second floor level with doors leading to the guest rooms. The stone chimney above the large stone hearth ran up through the roof at the peak. Somehow, we weren't surprised in this setting to see the huge stuffed head of a moose sporting six foot wide antlers over the mantle place.

A massive chandelier hung in the center of the room. Looking up, it was hard to figure out how they could change the light bulbs at that height above the floor. One entire single story wall was covered with cases crammed full of old, hardcover bound books. The hint of a saddle soap smell on aged leather emanated from the furniture positioned around the room on the faded oriental rugs that covered most of the highly polished hardwood floor.

From a closet shelf, Gord pulled out a holster, a box of shells, and a 9 mm, NATO compliant, general service pistol. He handed them to Jake and said, "Hopefully you won't need to use these."

Gord gave us a tour of the place and introduced us to Frenchy's wife, Gretchen, in the kitchen as we began salivating due to the heavenly potpourri of aromas of the foods being prepared. We were taken aback by the contrast to Frenchy because Gretchen was close to six feet tall with strong Teutonic features and braided flaxen hair. The fact that she was wearing a shoulder holster under her apron for her sidearm seemed to be contradictory to her overall appearance.

Her unaccented English didn't quite seem to fit with her physical image either when she said, "It's nice to meet you both. Please let us know if there's anything you need. Dinner will be ready in a few minutes. You must be hungry after your trip. I made lobster Newberg for dinner with apple strudel for dessert. There's a fresh pot of coffee on the stove when you're ready."

I said, "Thank you so very much, it's been a long day.

Ja… uh…I mean, Cliff would you like a cup of coffee?"

"Thank you, Brenda. I would love one. It smells great."

The newly christened Brenda and Cliff sat down with their coffee mugs as Frenchy and Gord poured coffee for themselves. Gretchen placed the plate of freshly baked biscuits and the tureen of lobster Newberg on the table and joined us. Having missed lunch, our eyes lit up at the sight of the food presented.

In between mouthfuls, Gretchen was praised for being more than successful with the dinner. Everyone ladled out a second generous helpings for themselves, and we almost grumbled about not having saved enough room for dessert, but the strudel looked and smelled too good to pass up.

Over dessert, Gord mentioned that a low orbit, X-47B prototype space plane was scheduled to pass overhead at 0600 hours to broadcast data bursts for downloading and decoding, so we should be up early enough for it.

After washing down the rest of our strudel with another cup of coffee, we pushed ourselves away from the table. Before retiring upstairs, we thanked the Canadians for their efforts to get us here safely and looking after us.

Getting out of our flight suits and clothes, Jake said, "You realize that this is the first time Brenda and Cliff have been alone together. It's kind of like their honeymoon."

As I took his hand and dragged him toward the bed, I responded with, "Well, we know each other a lot better than they do, so we don't have to be slow, careful, or shy. Come here, babe, the last time I had you was two countries ago." Having been uncoupled for what was an unusually long time for us, we went at it as fast and furiously as we dared while we made an effort not to make too much noise. Trying to catch my breath, I said, "Now you and I both know Brenda and Cliff could not possibly have enjoyed that as much as we did."

Satiated, we fell asleep exhausted and entwined in each other's arms until Jake's watch beeped in an annoying high pitched tone on the night stand. I asked, "What time is it?"

Fumbling for his watch on the nightstand with his eyes still closed, Jake managed to get one eye partially open. Squinting to focus, he said, "0500. I mean 5 AM. I'm starting to feel like I'm back in the military after the last two days. We need to get downstairs to see if we will receive any instructions on what comes next on the agenda they have laid out for us."

In an effort to wake up, we splashed water on our faces and tried to comb back our pillow hair, which was still matted down from the perspiration caused by the bed gymnastics of the previous evening.

As we stumbled down the stairs, we were surrounded by the delightful aroma arising from Gretchen's freshly brewed coffee mingling with the wonderful smells of Canadian bacon and home fries sizzling on the grill. Gord looked up from the PC screen and said, "Cliff, your eyes resemble two piss holes in the snow. Did you manage to get any sleep last night? Brenda on the other hand, looks lovely."

"Why thank you, Gord, and good morning, Gretchen," I said. Do they chain you to the stove or give you a little break now and then? Everything looks and smells delicious."

"As my grandparents used to say, 'Guten Morgen. Wie geht's,'" Gretchen said with a cheerful smile.

I responded in kind, "Gut, danke."

Jake announced, "I brought the flight suits down. I'll put them out of the way in the closet." Then he asked Gord, "How does the streamed coded satellite message work?"

Gord replied with, "I enter an instructional code on my computer to send a message to a larger unit behind a wall panel in an upstairs closet, telling it to decode the raw encrypted data and send it back to my PC for analysis. If an immediate answer is required, we only have a ten-minute window before the plane's transmission and reception capability is out of range. Otherwise, we have to wait until another one of the satellite repeaters is in position for us to respond. The time varies between communication windows. Go ahead and have breakfast; I'll let you know when the message starts coming in and if an answer is necessary."

Frenchy joined us as we started with the breakfast of French toast, scrambled eggs, bacon, and home fries. Jake turned around to look when he heard the printer start up.

Gord waved him off and typed in a couple of lines on the keyboard before executing the command for the reply to be automatically translated to code and sent. Then he came into the kitchen and dropped a printed page in front of us. As he poured another coffee and filled his plate, he said, "They want us to meet them at the British Consulate in Toronto at 0900 one week from today with Thomas Mallard, the British high commissioner, and Ronald Butler, British consul general. Colonel Picketing of MI6 will be there from London as will members of the CIA and my boss, Brigadier-General Pierre Richard. I sent a coded response we'd be there."

19

As he rose from the table after breakfast, Jake noticed a chessboard was set up in the corner and challenged Gord to a game. Frenchy followed them into the living room and sat down to kibitz. I finished up my second cup of coffee, helped Gretchen clear the table, and offered to dry since she had already begun washing the dishes. Gretchen said she was going out later for supplies and wanted to know if there was anything we required from the village. I told her I needed a deep brown hair color dye, and Jake would like a baseball cap from a local team, perhaps one with a Toronto Blue Jays' logo.

Gretchen drained the sink and put away the dishes I had dried with a towel and stacked on the counter. Grabbing her grocery list, she replaced her apron with a lightweight jacket. Stopping to look in the hallway mirror, she made certain the bulge from her gun holster wasn't that obvious.

Gord apparently was concentrating on the game when Gretchen asked him if there was anything, she could get for him in town.

He looked up and said, "Huh?" before it registered what she had said. Then he replied, "There's nothing I can think of, but thanks for asking." Turning his attention back to the chess game in progress, his wrinkled brow suggested he was disturbed by the fact that Jake was already ahead by a bishop and a knight.

Gretchen seemed to have been gone for some time, based on the fact that Jake and Gord had each won a game and were in the middle of setting up the pieces for a rubber match. I was just starting to read the second old magazine I had found in the living room when she pulled into the garage. Frenchy and I rose to lend her a hand bringing in the groceries from the SUV.

As she was putting everything away, Gretchen said she went to three different stores but couldn't locate a Blue Jays' cap. She did manage to find one with the Toronto Maple Leafs' emblem and several women's magazines for me to pass the time with, however.

Since Gord and Jake were still totally absorbed in their match, I said, "I'm sure the hat will be fine, but I'd like to get a picture of Jake with the Leafs' cap on next to the Maple Leaf Inn sign out in front before we leave."

Holding up a box, Gretchen said, "I picked out a Clairol Nice and Easy 004 Dark Brown permanent hair color for you. I hope that will be okay."

Looking at the color of the tint illustrated on the label, I said, "Thank you. That's perfect. Do you have a pair of scissors I could use to trim my hair?"

Gretchen responded, "Yes, I do. Would you like me to help?"

"That would be great. I wasn't sure I could cut the back by myself and make it come out even."

Gretchen found a plastic coated tablecloth to wrap around me, grabbed the box of hair color, and led me upstairs to one of the larger bathrooms. In no time at all, she had my hair trimmed to shoulder length, dyed brown, and blown dry.

My gaze shifted from the mirror down to the floor at my natural blond hair trimmings. They were covered with dark brown clips, cut when Gretchen evened the trim line off after the dye job. Then I was overwhelmed with mixed emotions to see a stranger when I looked back in the mirror. I had just given up my identity for what? To prevent someone I didn't know from attacking me on the chance I would be recognized?

Since the woman who was reflected back at me from the mirror didn't look like the me I was accustomed to seeing, perhaps the change in appearance would be drastic enough to keep me safe.

It just made me so mad that these few crazies could disrupt the lives of millions of people in the name of a religion they twisted out of shape, so it no longer resembled the Islamic faith they claimed to represent. Why couldn't the sane Muslims control their own people? Are they so frightened of their own weirdoes that we have to track them down? Knowing there are no answers to these questions, I had to get them out of my skull before I gave myself a headache.

Perhaps because I was sitting there staring at the mirror for so long, Gretchen asked, "Well, how do you like it Brenda?"

After a long pause, I said, "You did a wonderful job, but I haven't decided what I think of it yet. I've always been a blond with longer hair, and this is so different. It looks very nice but will probably take me a while to get acclimated to it. Thank you so much for your help."

After we cleaned up the bathroom, I led the way downstairs and into the living room. The chess tournament had apparently morphed into a more serious stage and was still in progress. As I stepped through the archway, Gord must have noticed me out of the corner of his eye. He jumped up, knocked the board over, and all the chess pieces flew off the table as he reached for his gun, shouting, "Who are you, and how did you get in here?"

I raised my hands over my head and screamed, "Gord, don't shoot. It's me, Brenda!"

Slowly, he lowered the pistol, still not quite sure if it really was me. By the time I was able to catch my breath with my rapid pulse finally beginning to slow down again, I noticed Jake's mouth was still wide open in disbelief. I must have slumped over, because I realized at last that Gretchen was supporting me from behind.

Gord's face had drained of color as he returned his gun back to his shoulder holster. His mouth seemed to be oddly distorted when he said, "Brenda, I'm sorry if I frightened you. We learn to act on reflex. Please warn me ahead of time if you're ever going to do something like that again."

Trying to collect my thoughts and composure, I said, "I guess I won't be easily recognized when it becomes time to leave here." My teeth were still chattering from fright as I added, "What do you think of the change Cliff?" just to say something.

"You certainly are still stunning as a brunette. It's just that you don't look like the woman I fell in love with," Jake replied. "I'm sure it will grow on me eventually though."

Since I seemed to be able to carry my own weight again, Gretchen stepped back and said, "That's enough excitement for one day. How about I make a fresh pot of coffee, and we can polish off the rest of the apple strudel leftover from yesterday?"

"Jake and Gord gathered up the chess men scattered all over the living room rug and wandered into the kitchen where Frenchy was sitting across the table from me, staring at my new hairdo. Stroking his chin in contemplation, he turned and asked, "Gretchen, have you ever considered trying a different hair color?"

Gretchen did a quick 180 pivot on one foot and glared daggers at him. Frenchy immediately cast his eyes downward at the table and didn't dare say another word.

The remainder of the strudel was expertly cut into precisely five equal pieces by Gretchen. All the while, Frenchy kept a keen eye on the knife she was using as if he expected it to fly in his direction without a moment's warning. Gretchen served the pastry on dessert plates and poured the coffee.

Jake suggested to Gord that he probably tipped the chess board over because he was behind, but they could do a rematch the next day, unless Frenchy wanted to play against him. Then the computer in the next room started to chatter.

Gord went into the living room to do his thing to decode the message and returned shortly with a hard copy. Handing it to me, he said, "This one's for you, Brenda."

I glanced at the first few paragraphs and said, "Cliff, could you please come upstairs with me to discuss this?"

Jake followed me to the bedroom and closed the door behind him. He asked, "What does it say?"

I told him he could see for himself as soon as I finished reading the first page. I handed that page to Jake while I read the other two.

In the middle of the page, Jake said, "Wow! I never would have believed it. It's about my Pakistani grad student who was doing a portion of the blind chemical analysis tests on the Quabbin water samples. He received a lump sum of Iranian oil money funneled through Singapore. He subsequently distributed part of the money to the seven Muslim chemical engineers my task force caught trespassing at the Quabbin Reservoir earlier this year. He might be the leader of the terrorist cell in Western Massachusetts.

"The CIA also found he was e-mailing his sister in Newton, Massachusetts. Maybe it was to obtain results of their reservoir trial runs on the Boston end. That could be how they figured out I was involved in the CIA effort to stop the Islamic plot to poison the water supply for the greater Boston area. It's a good thing you were able to get the names and contacts of the Far East banks from Leslie for the CIA to watch."

I said, "The third page says that money from the same account was also routed to a larger terrorist cell in Boston and another one in London. The CIA has begun reviewing the e-mail correspondence of the others."

Jake explained, "The Newton group has to be collecting samples on that end to determine dilution factors, flow times, and efficacy from the Quabbin spike tests that were showing up intermittently in Boston's tap water. If it wasn't from getting my name from the police report filed at the Quabbin Reservoir, they might have determined I was involved in trying to foil their plot based on the results of the test samples I was submitting for analyses. That probably means they were after me and didn't know about you or Leslie. At least I feel better about that."

"Oh, Jake, I don't. That means you probably are still a target."

"Maybe not, Pam. It says here the CIA is fairly certain they rounded up all the jihad cell members in Massachusetts and London. It's possible we're out of the woods in terms of not having to remain here in hiding," Jake said.

"Just the same, we need to be careful until we get the all-clear sign from the CIA," I said. "In the meantime, we'll assume it's business as usual, and we're stuck here for the duration until we see what's resolved at the British Consulate meeting in Toronto next week.

"Oh, I almost forgot. Gretchen found this Toronto Maple Leafs' cap in the village for you to wear in your Canadian passport and driver's license photos. With a beard and the cap, even I might not recognize you. It's funny, I feel like I'm still shaking. I've never had anyone point a gun in my direction before. Please come over here and hold me for a while until I can relax a little."

"Mmmm. You may look like Brenda now, but at least you still feel like my Pam when you snuggle up," Jake said, wrapping his arms around me and giving me a big squeeze. "I'm glad to know Pam is still in there under that brown hair."

"And don't you forget it, mister," I said, looking at him straight in the eye before sharing a prolonged, passionate kiss. "We'd better go downstairs before we start something we can't finish right now."

Gord looked up from his coffee and strudel to see us coming down the stairs. "What's the verdict? Do we need a response for the message?"

"No, not yet," I said. "It was mostly informative, but it was good news. They're making progress on finding the enemy. I do need to contact M. Kent Clark, the CEO of Toronto Dominion Bank, at their headquarters in Toronto on a secure telephone line as soon as you can arrange it, though. Just explain a director of Grady Trading Company wishes to speak with him about a confidential matter."

Gord said, "I'll get right on that. Pardon me if I seem to be staring, but if I didn't know better, I'd swear you're a different person than you were earlier today. The change in your appearance is so dramatic from the way you looked before."

"That's probably a good thing in terms of not being recognized. Let's hope the baseball cap and a beard work well enough to disguise Cliff, so they won't be able to spot him either," I said.

"Good point. I'll see if I can scare up a realistic looking beard for Cliff while I'm at it. Then we can arrange to get your new IDs before we go out to the meeting next week," Gord said as he returned to work on his keyboard.

It was apparent that Gretchen still felt Frenchy was not happy with her appearance as a blond, so they were no longer on speaking terms. Every now and then, Frenchy would timidly raise his head to say something to Gretchen, but the icy cold stare she constantly projected kept him quiet.

Jake and I had returned to the kitchen table to finish our dessert when Gretchen turned with a big smile to pleasantly ask if we'd like more coffee.

I felt bad that Frenchy was being treated poorly by Gretchen because of a misunderstanding, but I returned her smile and said, "Yes, thank you. It was very good."

Jake asked if she could warm up his coffee and said the strudel was exceptional. Gretchen did a double take when Jake asked her for the recipe. He told her that his grandmother taught him how to make a Swedish tea ring with similar ingredients, but he'd like to see if he could make something that tastes anything close to being as delicious what she made.

Gretchen smiled and seemed genuinely flattered by his request. She proceeded to write out a copy translated to English from a well-worn, old recipe book written in German. She explained that the apple strudel recipe was handed down through the family for generations. Her grandmother brought it with her when the family immigrated to Canada. While Gretchen was busy writing at the table, Frenchy came up behind her, kissed her on the nape of the neck, and went out to the garage without saying a word.

Gord returned to the kitchen and said, "Mr. Clark is out today but is expected back in the morning. I have arranged for a secure telephone link with TD Bank headquarters through the Canadian Security Intelligence Service's switchboard in

Ottawa. Mr. Clark's executive administrator will be expecting your call at nine tomorrow morning.

"It so happens, the undercover group at CSIS has a retired makeup artist on call for our field operatives. Frenchy will pick her up tomorrow to fit Cliff with a beard and show him how to put it on until his own beard grows out more."

Gretchen had been setting up the sideboard cupboard in the kitchen with her freshly baked rye bread, thinly sliced corn beef, lettuce, tomatoes, onions, and condiments for a fix it yourself dinner. Pausing a minute in thought, she went out to find Frenchy working on his antique car in the far end of the multi-bay garage. Whatever words were exchanged must have patched things up because they came into the kitchen holding hands and grinning like a couple of teenagers on their first date.

After we all ate our fill, we filed into the living room to catch up on the world news. Since there didn't appear to be much of interest on the satellite dish TV system after that, Jake and I bade everyone a good evening and retired upstairs to our bedroom.

I pushed the door shut, engaged the antique wrought iron dead bolt, and drew Jake up close. Looking up into those intense blue eyes, I asked Jake if he had any fantasies. He put his arms around me and said that while it might be easy to imagine he was with someone else since my change in appearance was indeed radical, I was the only one he had ever wanted. Then he asked if I ever had any fantasies.

I told him, "I fantasize about you all the time. Even when you're only across the room, I daydream about how wonderful it will be when we can be together later in the evening."

He said with a grin and a mischievous twinkle in his eye, "I'm glad you told me, so I can be on the alert in case you try to attack me in the middle of the day." Without saying another word, Jake tenderly swooped me up in his arms. He then placed me gently on the bed where he proceeded to undress me ever so slowly, kissing me all over...

The following day, we went down to the kitchen with the lure of a cloud of freshly brewed coffee aroma leading the way. We said good morning to Gord and Frenchy just before Gretchen came sashaying down the hall with a smug expression on her face, wearing a dressy outfit and high heels. Without her apron and holster, she looked like a fashion model after letting her braided hair down and wearing makeup with lipstick for a change. Frenchy said, "Wow, do you ever look gorgeous, ma cherie," adding quickly, "Not that you didn't before of course." This precipitated a chorus of unrestrained laughter after the misunderstanding of the previous day.

When the chuckles finally subsided, Jake said, "Gretchen, I agree. You do look absolutely lovely today." After a brief pause, he added, "But then again, you look lovely in an apron with a weapon under your arm too." At which point, we broke out laughing all over again, which caused Frenchy to erupt with coffee coming out of his nose. Being a good sport, Gretchen couldn't keep a straight face and laughed right along with us.

Gretchen apparently had already mixed the pancake batter and preheated the grill before we came down to breakfast. She deftly ladled out a half dozen buttermilk pancakes at a time on the grill and had a couple of stacks on the table before our coffee was cool enough to sip. She poured syrup into the decanters on the table from a gallon jug with a huge maple leaf on the label, probably just to let us know it was a Canadian product. She managed to do all this with a friendly smile and without spilling a drop of syrup or batter on what appeared to be a brand-new dress.

20

Following breakfast, Gord set up the secure telephone line to the TD Bank CEO routed through the Canadian Intelligence Service switchboard in Ottawa. By the appointed hour of nine, we had a connection established with Mr. Kent Clark. I said, "Hi, Kent. This is Pam Mullen of Grady Trading Company."

Kent said, "Hello, Pam, great to hear from you again. How can I be of assistance?"

I said, "I apologize for the cloak and dagger subterfuge, but the CIA is having difficulty dealing through intergovernmental channels concerning the Newton branch of your Canadian bank near Boston. While I'm sure it can be resolved, time is of the essence. They have asked me to see if I couldn't intervene on their behalf to expedite the process. They need to obtain the financial transaction records of what we believe is an Islamic terrorist cell operating out of Newton, Massachusetts.

"Oh dear, that doesn't sound good at all. Not to worry about the formalities and regulations though. We can let the appropriate paperwork and documentation catch up later. I'll contact the branch manager immediately and ask her to provide all the necessary information while exercising the utmost discretion," he said. "Her name is Beverly Cadman. Will you be the one calling, or will it be someone else?"

"It will be a Ms. Taylor Young of the CIA in Langley, Virginia," I said. "Thank you so much, Kent. Please give my regards to Lois. I'll try to catch you again the next time I'm up in your area."

"Glad to help, Pam. Except for the circumstances, it was nice to hear your lovely voice again. Please don't be a stranger," he said.

After hanging up, I hand wrote a short message and asked Gord to relay it as soon as possible to Taylor Young of the CIA in Langley through the American Embassy here in Canada.

I was relieved that matter was successfully resolved, but later that day, Gord received another coded message from Manny of the CIA. This one was addressed to Jake with a heading of "Top Secret."

Again, we retreated to the bedroom to see what this one was all about. Jake must have been puzzled after he determined it was a final report on the results of his last water sampling from the Quabbin Reservoir because he started to read it from the beginning again when he had finished.

After the second review, Jake still looked perplexed, so I asked him why he looked so confused.

He said, "I was astonished to learn that the reservoir samples contained inorganic arsenic salt particulates, encapsulated in an organic micro foam, which reduced the composite specific gravity to just above one. That would cause them to float several feet down in the water yet prevent them from sinking to the bottom. Eventually, they would be transmitted to Boston via the pipeline.

"That explained how the arsenic compound was able to escape inclusion by the normal surface sampling technique or settle harmlessly to the bottom of the reservoir. The toxin floated well below the standard test depths of the water in the reservoir. The coated arsenic salt would not dissolve until acted upon by stomach acid after ingestion. This eliminated chance detection in the Quabbin or Wachusett Reservoirs. The quantities involved in the test runs were so diluted; the pollutants could have been easily overlooked when sampled from a tap in Boston.

"We were fortunate to have taken the specimens in shallow water before they were diluted, caught in the current and swept out where the water was deeper, so timing was serendipitous in this case. Full scale contamination would probably not have been detected until millions of people started to die off at the same time unless Boston caught up on their backlog of routine analyses. With the current level of understaffing at the Massachusetts State Laboratories, the chance of a catastrophe of that order of magnitude being detected early enough to be prevented was miniscule."

"If your Quabbin team hadn't been able to figure out what these fanatics were doing, how many people would have been affected?" I asked.

Jake replied, "There are well over a half million people in metropolitan Boston, but an additional two million users in the forty towns surrounding Boston also depend exclusively on water from the Quabbin Reservoir. When you consider that half of the water from the Quabbin pipeline leaks out in transit and add in the overflow from the Windsor Dam, contamination of the Quabbin and the abutting aquifers could collectively poison over six million people in Massachusetts, Connecticut, Rhode Island, and New Hampshire."

"That's a big threat to a lot of innocent people due to a misinterpretation of the Koran by a few relatively small groups of vicious tribal nomads who want to blame their woes on the rest of the world. How are we going to prevent something like this from happening in the future?" I asked.

"The forty square miles of the Quabbin reservoir has 180 miles of shoreline patrolled by the police. My task team has only caught the one group of seven foreign nationals trespassing after dark thus far, but it's obvious that additional restrictive measures are necessary. Who knows how many times they've been there before, and how many unauthorized visits by other people went undetected?

"A major step up in the frequency of patrols will be required to secure the reservoir. Access will need to be restricted further. A system of motion activated cameras will have to be installed and constantly monitored, coupled with drone surveillance."

"It sounds like the cost of vigilance will result in considerable expenses and additional losses of personal liberties," I said.

Jake said, "That's what happens when we have a revolving door policy on immigration without adequate screening on who we let into the United States. The fishing, hunting, and bird watching privileges of a miniscule percentage of the population has to be trumped by the welfare of the millions of people in southern New England who interface with the water from western Massachusetts. The rest of the people in Massachusetts subsidize greater Boston's water supply and waste treatment costs. Until that situation changes, there are no incentives for them to finish cleaning up the rivers and lakes for potable water supplies in eastern Massachusetts, which could be protected more effectively."

I asked Jake what the next step for him would be.

He replied, "They want me to confirm the estimates for the quantities of toxins involved up to this point. Then they'd know what kind and size of vehicles to be on the alert for. My temporary replacement, Rick Nugent, came up with ballpark figures, so I'll just double check his numbers."

"Jake, this is becoming far too dangerous. I've been extremely frightened ever since you were attacked, and they were shooting at us when we were being chased around Hyde Park in London. Now that we've finally found one another, I don't want to take a chance on losing you. Please tell me you'll quit your CIA activities as soon as we get out of this predicament," I pleaded.

"I don't know if I can leave the CIA and not finish what I started without handing it over as an organized package to someone else first. Then they won't have to start from scratch the way I did," Jake said. "If I'm still in danger when we're ready to get out of here, they will probably make allowances and let me off the hook, but I did take an oath to serve."

"Just promise me that you will try to let someone else take over for you as soon as you can," I begged. "I love you too much to see you hurt or worst."

"Maybe they'll consider letting me go since I'm officially only approved for 'limited duty' because of my back, but I can only try," Jake said as he gave me a kiss.

Jake went to do a few calculations and gave Gord a reply that said a panel van with an eight-foot bed could hold enough fiber drums to produce measurable test results in Boston. Based on the relatively low apparent density of the fluffy powder, the containers would be light enough for a crew of two or three people to roll through the woods and dump in the water without leaving a trace of activity near the shoreline.

Just when we thought everything had settled down so we could catch our breath, Frenchy showed up at the inn with the retired makeup artist, Shannon Quinn. After careful examination of Jake's face, the third beard and mustache combination she pulled from her kit was an exact match to the stubble on his chin.

Under her careful direction, she had Jake apply the adhesive, mount the bushy beard, and comb it in place to simulate the natural growth patterns on the contours of his face. I was surprised Jake was totally transformed in appearance as Cliff once he donned his new Toronto Maple Leafs' cap.

Shannon said there was one problem. The hat would help conceal his identity, but it wouldn't be permitted for the driver's license and passport photographs. She went back to her kit again and extracted a wig to match the beard, which would cover up his short, military style haircut until that grew out. She stepped back after integrating it with the beard and combing it out. Following her careful study, she nodded to signify her approval.

I wasn't expecting it, but Shannon turned around, looked at me, and said, "You're next, Brenda." From her magic box of tricks, she proceeded to do a makeover on me with darker eyebrow pencil, makeup, and lipstick to match my now dark colored hair. By combing my hair forward slightly with the strategic application of blush to make my cheekbones seem lower, my face suddenly appeared to be gaunt. When Shannon had finished, she handed me a mirror. With the brown hair dye job and the trim Gretchen had done before, my look was different. But now with the newly shaped brows, shading and deeper complexion, even I didn't recognize me.

Shannon reached into her box to produce a Polaroid camera, so she could take pictures for Brenda's and Cliff's driver's licenses and passports. With that accomplished, she demonstrated to Jake how to use the solvent to remove the beard and left the makeup behind that she'd used on me.

The following day, Gord went to Ottawa and returned with Canadian licenses and passports for Brenda and Clifford MacOmber of the village of Hope in Vaughan, Ontario. I had an eerie feeling run down my spine, looking at the IDs of these two people. They didn't even resemble distance relatives of ours, yet we shared the same birthdays with them, eh?

The rest of week seemed to go surprisingly fast. Jake kept Gord busy by sending frequent encoded messages to Manny of the CIA and translating the replies. That was over and above all the coded exchanges of financial tracking information I had with Taylor. On an as needed basis, Gord also kept me in contact with my business associates on secure lines through his security headquarters in Ottawa and the American Embassy.

In between all the communication operations, we happened to find out Gretchen and Frenchy knew how to play bridge. We thought this would be a perfect way to pass the time in between the spurts of intense activity while we were waiting for the satellite's next low orbital broadcast.

I hadn't played since my college days in the sorority, but it all came back fairly quickly. Jake had never learned how to play, but he was a quick study. At first Jake would team up with Frenchy, and Gretchen would be my partner against the guys.

After a couple of days, the contests of the guys against the girls seemed to be almost equally matched. Being an instinctively aggressive bidder, Jake played and won more than his share of games. If a few of the finer points of bidding conventions were employed, the scores could have been higher, but it was a fun break in the tedium of waiting. It was also a welcome distraction from the potentially dangerous situation, which we found ourselves entrapped in.

It wasn't long before Jake and I were both up to speed, and it became a case of the Canadians teaming up against the Americans. It occurred to me that was a strange way of putting it since the Canadians are North Americans, the same as we are. Playing bridge certainly helped to pass the time, so we didn't feel so isolated out in the Ontario countryside either.

In the meantime, Gord verified that everything was proceeding as scheduled for the meeting at the British Consulate's office in Toronto. A decoded message addressed to me from Taylor at the CIA said, according to Walter Pickering at MI 6 in London, the brother of the Saudi who attacked Jake in London was the recipient of jihad funds processed by another source in Singapore that Longstaff of Barclays Bank had identified.

Once captured, he had been worn down by sleep deprivation and was "singing like a canary," as she put it. Through his e-mails and computer records, they were able to establish electronic and money trails of all three groups of troublemakers in London, Boston, and western Massachusetts involved in the Boston water adulteration attempts.

Together with the financial records Taylor had obtained from the TD Bank branch in Newton, Massachusetts, she was able to fill in all the missing pieces. Taylor said they all had been captured, and everyone at their base in Yemen had been eliminated with two coordinated drone attacks.

The purpose of that particular coded message appeared to be purely informative, but I suspect Taylor wanted to allay my fears while letting me know that this was made possible by our joint efforts.

21

When the day of the Toronto meeting finally rolled around, I tried to remember exactly how Shannon had applied and spread each cosmetic layer. The final result wasn't even close to the perfection of the professional job Shannon had done, but I did resemble my new passport photograph enough not to draw unwanted attention by airport security.

The time it took Jake to glue and groom his beard elapsed so much faster by comparison; he kept walking by the bathroom to see what could possibly be taking me so long. It was obvious he didn't dare say anything to interrupt me, knowing it would then take even longer for me to finish getting ready if I was nervous or distracted.

Gord and Frenchy were patiently waiting as we came down the stairs in our Brenda and Cliff personae, once the transformations were complete. Gord tried to keep a straight face as he looked up and posed the question, "Who *are* these people?"

I said, "Gord, the last time you watched me come down the stairs, you looked like you planned to shoot on sight. Thank you for using more restraint and better judgment this time."

As he led the way to the garage, Gord said with a smile, "Next time I'll ask you for the password and secret handshake to make certain it's really you."

After being confined for over a week in a safe house, it was nice to see the countryside again, even though it was through the tinted windows of the SUV on the way to downtown Toronto. As exciting as all this adventure had been, it wasn't what I signed up for. After almost twenty years, I walked away from what I thought was my ideal position as a professional to be with the love of my life, and what happened?

Being free to see the sunshine, trees, and grass I once took for granted felt like a treat. I can only be with Jake with others around to protect us and need a disguise to go out in public. I've lost my identity. All my friends and contemporaries in the business world wouldn't recognize me if they bumped into me on the street. I'm frightened that I might be attacked by someone with a warped or no sense of values, who doesn't even know me. I've been able to shut that out of my mind for the most part. What I can't forget is that these crazy people have already tried to kill Jake, and he still is a target. Jake has become my reason for being, and I don't know what I would do if I ever lost him.

Jake noticed the deep frown lines on Pam's forehead and gave her a kiss. He smiled down at her, put his arm around her shoulder, and reached out to take her hand. *Jake, you're an idiot,* he said to himself. *Here you've found a wonderful woman you want to spend the rest of your life with, and you let her volunteer to put her life in danger.* Then and there, he made a promise to himself that if and when they get out of this predicament unscathed, he would make certain that she'd be safe and secure for as long as she'd put up with him.

I looked up at Jake, smiled, snuggled a little closer, put my head back against Jake's shoulder, closed my eyes, and gave his hand a squeeze.

Upon our arrival at the office of the British Consulate, Jake and I were led to a separate conference room from the registration area by CIA agents Taylor Young and Manny Rodriquez. As soon as the door closed, Taylor said, "I can't believe it's you two. I wouldn't have been able to pick either one of you out of a lineup. Now I will have to remember to call you Brenda and Cliff. I'm so glad to see you made it here without incident."

Turning serious, Special Agent Young read the statement from Leon Spinetti, Director of the CIA addressed to Jacob Wells and Pamela Mullen.

"The CIA has been authorized by Natalie Gaudette, secretary of Homeland Security, to inform you that Islamic terrorist sleeper cells were uncovered in the UK, the United States, and Yemen because of the financial tracking information and methodology supplied by Pamela Mullen. This had a direct impact on the work done by the task force directed by Jacob Wells to prevent the direct poisoning of the water supplies for the millions of households in the greater Boston area and contamination of the many aquifers in southern New England, which abut the pipeline or are downstream of the reservoir overflows.

"Due to the efforts of the Toxic Pollutant Tracking Team, under the leadership of Jacob Wells, in place at the Quabbin Reservoir and Boston, a terror cell in western Massachusetts and a much larger one in the Metropolitan Boston area were located. All the individuals in both groups have been taken into custody. We believe all the members of the terrorist cells involved in this undertaking in the United States, and England have been captured. Interrogation is still ongoing, but you should no longer be in any danger. Their al-Qaida associates in Yemen have been neutralized.

"Although your contributions can't be publicly announced as to what was accomplished or how due to national security concerns, the president has asked us to convey his heartfelt thanks and express his deepest gratitude for jobs well done on behalf of the American people. It was noted that the Saudi terrorist captured in London was in fact, after Mr. Jacob Wells. It seems they were not aware of Ms. Pamela Mullen's involvement or that of her business associates who provided support."

Following pats on the back, high fives, and handshakes from Taylor and Manny, we adjourned to the main conference room.

22

As we entered the room, I spotted and pointed out Colonel Walter Pickering in the middle of the officials milling about.

Jake immediately went over to tap him on the shoulder as I followed. Jake asked Walter, "Excuse me, sir, but are you acquainted with a former United States army captain by the name of Jacob Wells?"

Walter turned and said, "Yes, as a matter of fact I am. He's expected soon. And who might you be?"

"Someone you wouldn't recognize in a crowd, Walter. It's me, Jake, but you can call me Cliff MacOmber," he said in a hushed voice with the open palm of his hand next to Walter's ear as he leaned in closer to whisper.

Walter took one step back to look Jake up and down. "Really?" he replied.

Jake whispered, "No kidding, Walter. This is my disguise until we're certain I'm no longer a target for the bad guys."

"I wouldn't have guessed in a million years. And this couldn't possibly be Pamela, your lovely, formerly blonde partner?" Walter said.

"As you can see, she's now a gorgeous brunette. Walter, I'd like to introduce you to Cliff MacOmber's new bride, Brenda," Jake said.

"Now you've got to be pulling my leg, old boy. I can't believe this is the same beautiful woman I met in London," he said, taking a cue from Jake to keep his voice low to avoid being overheard. Then in a more normal speaking tone, "I'm pleased to make your acquaintance, Mrs. MacOmber."

"It's a pleasure to meet you, Colonel Pickering. Please feel free to call me Brenda." I said, smiling while doing a little curtsy. "In that case, Brenda, please call me Walter," he said, trying his best to suppress a grin without having much success.

Walter said he wondered why he didn't see our names on the list of attendees for this meeting, but was still shaking his head when he said, "I assume this was the CIA's doing, but it probably makes sense for both of you to remain undercover for your safety, even with this group of high level dignitaries. Who knows where prying eyes might come across documentation from this meeting if a computer gets hacked?"

Walter had us accompany him to the corner of the room where he introduced his commander, Brigadier General Sheldon and Dennis Hisorie, the British ambassador to Canada. The general said to call him James and thanked us for our work in uncovering the Islamic plots that could have negatively impacted both of our countries. Mr. Hisorie said he had heard about our contributions to help thwart the plans of the al-Qaeda affiliated cells in London and the States, and we should contact him if there was any way he could serve as a liaison for us with the officials in London.

Major Gordon McNulty came over to inform us the meeting was about to convene if we wanted to pour ourselves a cup of coffee beforehand. No sooner were we seated when introductions of everyone were made around the table. Of course, the names and functions of the officials we didn't-already know all went by so fast, they were like a blur, so it was impossible to connect them with faces.

As Taylor approached the podium with a purposeful stride, I couldn't help but notice how well she filled out her two-piece pants suit. There was no chance she might be mistaken for a male because she was endowed with a voluptuous shape. Her muscle tone and carriage suggested the strength and courage of a mountain lion. As she walked, she projected determination and a certain air of self confidence.

Taylor was the first to speak since her group at the CIA had initiated the investigation into the banks in Hong Kong and Singapore from the list I had obtained from Barclays Bank. This resulted in the discovery of the oil money trails through Asia funneled to Islamic cells in Canada, America, and Brittan (CAB). She further indicated that the full cooperation of the CAB alliance's military, government, and institutions was crucial to locating and capture of the terrorists.

Taylor deftly punched the keyboard of her laptop as she showed the web-like diagram displayed on the wall screen with red lines radiating out from the Asian banks to the underground European and North American cells where the Arab oil money was dispersed to the terrorists. Taylor had a resonant alto voice with perfect enunciation that any evening news anchor would envy. She held the notable dignitaries' rapt attention while she carefully explained the details of the operations.

Taylor then said, "Just so everyone knows who they've been talking to on the phone and communicating with via e-mails, first I'd like to introduce Walter Pickering of MI6 in London. Colonel, please stand and accept our thanks for a job well done." This was followed by a round of applause.

Taylor continued, "Thank you, colonel. Now I'd like to introduce Major Gordon MacNulty who has been coordinating the Canadian security effort from their base in Ottawa."

When the applause subsided, Taylor paused to take a sip of water and said, "Because fringe elements of the Islamic faith have declared jihad on everyone else, we are hereby establishing a counter-terrorist effort called the War Against Radical Muslims or WARM for short. As other nations join in the WARM effort, we plan to make it as hot as possible for these insaniacs, so they have no place left on the globe to hide. "The CIA is confident that all those responsible for endangering the health and welfare of the people in New England have been rounded up and they are still being interrogated. Consequently, the United States will be reviewing our immigration policies and working with other countries to improve information sharing and transfer."

The critical data exchanges generated with the help of Canada and the United Kingdom foiled the nefarious Muslim plot to poison the Quabbin Reservoir water supply in Massachusetts. Had the terrorists' plan succeeded, it could have resulted in infinitely more deaths than 911 and impacted far beyond an order of magnitude more people than the three hundred thousand threatened by the toxic chemical spill in West Virginia's Elk River earlier this year. Taylor ended by thanking the Canadians and the Brits for providing safe havens for the Central Intelligence Agency advisors after they came under attack.

Pickering followed with a discussion of the terrorist group capture operation in London. While he was confident that all the individuals had been accounted for, interrogations were ongoing there as well. Because of the Asian banking information gleaned, the Yemen connection was also uncovered and neutralized by the United States Air Force drones.

Gord was next up to speak for Canadian Intelligence. He said he just learned that a sting operation at another bank in Singapore revealed two al-Qaeda affiliated Islamic groups operating in Calgary and Edmonton, Alberta were stockpiling large quantities of fuel drums and skids of fertilizer in both cities for the assumed purpose of building larger versions of the 1995 bomb detonated in Oklahoma City.

He suggested we might want to consider limiting just how much detailed information the media of our respective countries should be allowed to air or print about disasters such as that one or where to garner information on how to build a bomb.

It was suspected that the objective of this Muslim plan was to execute a coordinated attack to cripple Canada's oil industry and make a statement to the world that no place can be safe by putting a significant dent in the American oil supply. Accounting for 15 percent of US imports, Canada is the largest single oil supplier to the United States. It was hoped that the ongoing investigation would be concluded soon to assure everyone involved had been identified and arrested.

After his statements, Gord noted that the newly acquired financial tracking techniques supplied to the CIA by Brenda MacOmber were responsible for the recent success at ferreting out the terrorists in Alberta.

The group in the meeting then stood as one to applaud me.

When I was asked to say a few words, my face felt warm, and I must have blushed since I wasn't accustomed to this kind of praise for just doing my job at Grady Trading. With all the effort that went into my change of identity to avoid recognition, it seemed strange to be the focal point of the group's attention.

I advised them that the CIA only needed to modify a few of their existing techniques to upgrade their methodology previously in use. I also emphasized that I relied on cherry picking input from a network of numerous business acquaintances established over many years, that were spread around the globe, to assemble the necessary information. I further explained that the normally proprietary trade information was obtained based on trust built up over a long period of time because of my prior experience in dealing with all these people. Even though they were not made aware of exactly what I was trying to accomplish, they agreed to help with the understanding that they would remain anonymous. I pointed out that I gave them that assurance and promised not to reveal my sources so as not to put them in any danger.

It was determined at the meeting that Taylor Young, Walter Pickering, and Gordon MacNulty would be the primary coordinators for their respective countries on the WARM program. The consensus was that the United States and the United Kingdom would provide assistance to the Canadians in routing out the radicals involved in the Alberta plot. It was agreed that the CAB Alliance countries would work with Interpol to ferret out their Muslim counterparts in the Middle East and Asia.

Walter Pickering then said he recognized that the assembled group had no voice in the CIA's choice of personnel; but he wanted to make an unofficial motion anyway that Cliff and Brenda MacOmber be recruited to become full time undercover CIA agents. The motion was wholeheartedly seconded by Gordon MacNulty, followed by a chorus of hear, hears, and another standing ovation.

Once again I felt like I was turning a beet red, hiding my face in my hands. Jake and I had already decided that we wanted to be free to enjoy our lives together. While the accolades were nice, I hated to disappoint all these people who seemed to think we could solve all their problems. Surely they could find capable replacements for us in the battle to secure world peace.

When order had been restored to the meeting of the gathered officials and dignitaries, Taylor stood to announce that an in-depth discussion with the MacOmbers was next on the CIA agenda after this meeting was adjourned.

After completing detailed lists of tasks required for additional intelligence gathering to wrap up necessary actions against the plots to blow up the Alberta oil fields and to poison greater Boston's water supply, the initial Toronto WARM Summit Meeting was declared a success.

23

A new meeting convened in another conference room with Taylor and Manny from the CIA along with Gord representing the host country to discuss our situation. Because Colonel Pickering had been involved since the start of the effort, he was included to represent the interests of the United Kingdom.

Taylor said she had been assured that all the Muslims involved in both plots had been rounded up. Until final confirmation by all involved, she recommended that we return to the Maple Leaf safe house in the village of Hope for at least another week. Gord agreed and said that Canadian Intelligence would continue to provide the necessary support to guarantee our safety.

Next, Taylor looked at us with a big smile and said the CIA had already discussed proposing that we join their organization full time. Because everyone was more than pleased with the outcome of our efforts and convinced that it wouldn't have happened without our input and leadership, no one dissented. The CIA would be willing to work something out that was fully acceptable to both of us.

I was invigorated by our joint accomplishments and found this whole adventure absolutely thrilling, but I could no longer tolerate not knowing if Jake would be safe from one day to the next. I turned to Jake to let him do the talking since he had been dealing with the CIA much longer than I had.

Jake seemed to read my mind and said, "We've done what we could for our country and have been working toward finding a life of our own. If this all is satisfactorily resolved so we can return to being ordinary citizens, our plan is to teach at Dana University in the fall, period."

I suspect Taylor already knew what we wanted to do, but she quickly added, "We don't need an answer today. Please think it over and let us know if you would reconsider a role in our efforts in either a full or part-time capacity. We feel you both have exceptional talents and capabilities that would be extremely valuable in protecting our national security."

With that, Taylor said, "We know you've been cooped up in the safe house and could use a change of scenery. We've reserved a private room in a restaurant of the Little Italy section of Toronto called Café Diplomatico that Major MacNulty recommended."

Gord piped up with, "Make sure you save room for dessert. Toronto Life voted their cannoli the best in the city. Most people don't realize it, but there are more Italians in Canada than French."

I said, "I haven't had a chance to eat at an Italian restaurant in downtown Toronto for several years. That sounds wonderful."

"I guess I'll have to figure out how to get food past this full beard and mustache. Talk about a learning curve. At least nobody will be able to recognize us with our disguises as Brenda and Cliff MacOmber," Jake said.

As we all filed out the back door of the consulate to the parking area, Frenchy was waiting outside with the SUV to drive us the few blocks to College Street.

During the meal, Gord and Walter discovered they both served in the same areas of Afghanistan with Jake at different times. Once they started to compare notes on Jake's antics and the practical jokes he had played on his fellow soldiers, the tales shifted to his brave actions on the battlefield. At that point, Jake appeared to desperately want to change the subject as he nervously fiddled with his silverware and gulped water from his glass. I'd never known Jake to be modest about anything, but he seemed to be embarrassed to have two of his closest comrades in arms talk about his deeds. Apparently, he thought nothing about his personal safety when he protected and retrieved his fellow soldiers who were wounded in combat while he was under heavy enemy fire.

Every time Jake would break into the discussion about another aspect of serving in Afghanistan, the topic would drift back to Jake's heroics. Finally, Jake's solution was to look around to locate a restroom, but the conversation was still ongoing when he returned to the table. The reaction from Taylor and Manny was pure amusement due to Jake's strong objections at having his stories of valor recounted.

Walter was having trouble trying to remember to call us Brenda and Cliff, even though it didn't really matter when he slipped and called us Pamela and Jake in front of Gord or the CIA. Except for Jake being frustrated in attempting to open his mouth wide enough to get food past his full beard and mustache, we shared a delightful dinner in a very charming setting with pleasant company.

Gord then reached into his pocket and extracted tickets to the performance of Les Misérables playing at the Princess of Wales Theatre on King Street. It was just the kind of diversion we all needed to draw our minds off the terrorists and completely relax for a change.

We all thoroughly enjoyed the musical and said our goodbyes to Walter, Manny, and Taylor when Frenchy dropped them back at the British Consulate before we returned to the Maple Leaf Inn. The trip felt much shorter this time, and it almost seemed as though we were going home since we had spent so much time there.

Upon our arrival at the inn, we said good night and retired to our bedroom. Jake and I sat down to discuss what we were going to tell Taylor and Manny if and when we were assured we would be no longer in danger from the unstable Islamists who had targeted Jake. We both were certain we didn't want to become agents, or operatives on a regular basis. We especially didn't want to spend any additional time working undercover for the CIA.

I said, "Jake, you've done more than your share for the military. You were the recipient of the Purple Heart to prove it, and you still have the pain from shell fragments in your spine to serve as a daily reminder. Then you worked for the CIA as a part-time agent in charge of the Quabbin Reservoir Task Force to protect greater Boston's water supply. That involved all your free time when you weren't teaching, so you had no life of your own. I think you've done more than enough for the country. When do you get a turn to have fun for a change?"

"You're right, Pam. Jake said, "When I left the military, it seemed as though I still could do more to help bring down the bad guys. Maybe it was a sense of duty or the fact that I still had a void in my life that needed filling, but that was before we met. I do have a nagging feeling in my gut that I'm leaving the Quabbin Task Force work unfinished though."

"Jake! Someone else can see to that. You know that in the beginning, I agreed to become a consultant for the agency, but we ended up trapped as if we were virtual prisoners, hiding in a safe house. That prevented us from even enjoying our first vacation together we had planned.

"At first we thought I was the target but later realized that they were after you in the London attack. Unfortunately, there was no way to be sure I wasn't in danger as well or my business associates around the world whom I had sought out to obtain current information on world trends in financial transfers. In the end, we decided that if we both got out of this predicament alive, we wanted to pare down and simplify our lives to be able to enjoy them together. I'm holding you to that."

"Come here and hold me to you," Jake said. "We were working under the assumption that all the jihadists involved in trying to poison the drinking water in New England and blowing up the Alberta oil fields had been rounded up or accounted for. If that's the case, then the only additional action needed is to check on your appointment as a professor at the Dana University School of Business in Irving. The CIA appeared to desperately want us to extend our involvement with their organization, but we've told them multiple times, there was no way we would consider doing that. We decided you would immediately draft a letter of intent to Dean Brytowski to teach starting in the fall semester, if the opening hadn't been filled."

24

We all slept in late the next day after the musical play. Over a light breakfast of coffee and toast, I composed the note to Dean Brytowski to confirm my availability for the fall semester. Gord sat quietly at the other end of the table looking at his coffee mug. He didn't appear to be any more awake than we were, so I waited until his eyes seemed to be fully open before I asked him to forward the message to Dana University through the usual secure channels. He said it would be no problem, and he'd take care of that right after he finished breakfast.

Jake was perusing the sports section of the Boston Globe Newspaper that Frenchy had picked up for him when we were in the meeting at the British Consulate. He asked Gord if he could pull in any of the TV stations in the States up here. Gord said that would be no problem and asked what was he interested in. Jake said he had noticed that the New England Patriots were playing their first preseason game against the Denver Broncos, and it started in a few moments.

It didn't take long for Gord to locate the pre-game show with the satellite dish system. Soon Jake, Gord, and Frenchy were glued to the screen as Tom Brady took turns with Payton

Manning marching their respective teams up and down the playing field.

Gretchen apparently knew exactly what was needed to keep them happy and out from underfoot for the duration of the game. I gave her a hand carrying the beer, pretzels, chips, and dip into the living room. Except for leaning one way or another to avoid missing any of the action as we put the drinks and snacks on the coffee table in front of them, I don't know if any of the men really noticed we were even in the room.

Gretchen signaled for me to follow her back into the kitchen. Then she pulled out a deck of cards and a cribbage board from a cabinet. Once in a while the guys would yell at the players and referees. They would also cheer when the right team had a big play or scored. Other than that, it apparently was extremely important stuff, and one could only hear the commentators describing the action on the football field in between the cheers of the crowd. It didn't seem to matter that it was only a preseason game that wouldn't even count in the standings. It must have something to do with the gladiator gene that Gretchen and I don't seem to possess.

Cribbage, on the other hand, brought out the competitive side of me, especially when Gretchen was getting all the good card combinations and had skunked me on the previous game. The tide was finally turning for me when Gretchen excused herself to bring another round of drinks for the guys and to refill their snack bowls.

Gretchen returned to our game, and I asked, "How did you know they were running low on supplies?"

"After a few years of marriage, you develop a sixth sense about the timing on these things," Gretchen said.

"How did you happen to meet Frenchy?" I asked casually, trying not to appear too nosey.

Gretchen said, "Actually, it was right here at the Maple Leaf Inn. We were both working on separate cases and ended up in the same location at the same time. Afterward, we were both waiting for our new assignments when we went out for dinner and a movie in town together and one thing led to another...

Because of their silly no fraternization rules, our superiors weren't very happy with us when we told them we got married. In the final analysis, they decided that having us both stationed at the inn could be a good cover."

"And you don't get on each other's nerves being together all the time?" I asked.

"Well...as you noticed the other day, we do have an occasional misunderstanding, but all in all...we get along very nicely together," Gretchen replied.

"Were you able to get Frenchy to change the little things he does that annoy you or did you become accustomed to them?"

Gretchen thought for a minute and replied, "I probably do more things to perturb Frenchy than he does to bug me. I don't expect to have him change or want him to. That's part of what makes him who he is and why I love him so much."

"Maybe it's because I spent my whole life by myself until recently, but I'm accustomed to doing things my way without regard for anyone else. Now that Cliff is in the picture, I have to stop and think about how my decisions will affect him.

"Cliff's mind is like a sponge. He soaks in every bit of trivia he's ever been exposed to and feels he has to share it at every opportunity. Sometimes it can be annoying or overwhelming. Once in a while I'm tempted to give him a whack on the side of the head, but he has so many endearing qualities, I think I'll keep him after all," I said, smiling.

Gretchen replied, "I can tell that Cliff's is very much in love with you by the way he looks at you. I suspect he is more than willing to overlook any flaws you have. I'm also sure the last thing he would want to do is to annoy you on purpose. Perhaps you should take a personal inventory of any possible faults you might have and try to fix them for his sake."

"Do you worry about the danger involved in your line of work?" I asked.

Gretchen said, "It does get a little boring around here at times, but so far it's been much safer than the previous undercover jobs I've had for the government. Of course, there's always an element of risk involved, especially if the real reason for us being on the property were to be discovered, but we have means of contacting a nearby Royal Canadian Mounted Police (RCMP) barracks if we were under attack."

"Goodness gracious, Gretchen! Sorry, that sounded weird even to me, but that's both alarming and comforting at the same time. Now I'll have to try to erase that mental image of that happening from my brain. Maybe I'm just not cut out for this line of work. Do you have anything like an herbal tea to calm down my nerves?" I said as I looked down to see my hands trembling.

Gretchen said, "I'm sorry if I frightened you. After a while you learn to accept the potential danger as part of the job, and it doesn't bother you as much. I'll put water on the stove to brew the herbal tea right away."

Having changed the subject and nursed a cup of herbal tea, I had calmed down again by the time the football game was over. Gretchen had anticipated the guys would be ready for coffee and had a fresh pot prepared for them. Jake continued the discussion they were having as they entered the kitchen. He said, "I don't understand why the sportscasters and the sponsors go gaga over Peyton Manning when Brady has better statistics as he demonstrated by winning again today."

Gord replied, "It could be that the rest of the country is tired of watching the New England Patriots win, or Manning just has a better agent for getting parts in television commercials and publicity from the media."

A glance at Gretchen was all Frenchy needed to know not to continue the conversation about football, so to change the subject, he wisely asked, "So who won at cribbage?"

Gretchen replied, "Oh, we didn't keep track of the number of games we won. Cards are just something we do to keep our hands busy while we talk."

Gord added, "If that's the case, you probably don't want to hear any more football discussions, and I suspect we don't what to know what you girls talked about."

With a knowing grin and a wink, Jake turned to look at Gord and said, "You are wise well beyond your years, grasshopper," as he slapped him on the back.

"Speaking of which, I have something to discuss with you in private, Cliff," I said as I took Jake by the hand to lead him upstairs.

When we got to our room and closed the door, I said. "I was talking to Gretchen about how she handles the stress of not knowing from one minute to the next when and what kind of a threat will be encountered in assignments that she and Frenchy have to address. She said she was able to accept the risk, but she started in Canadian Intelligence by choice and felt good about being able to be of service to her country. Since she is together with Frenchy most of the time, she knows he's safe and doesn't need to worry about him that much."

Jake said, "I didn't have anyone to worry about me when I was in the army or after I began working undercover part time for the CIA. At the same time, I didn't have anyone to worry about or how my actions might affect them. Since you became involved with the CIA too, I think about it all the time, because the last thing I want to do is to put you in a dangerous situation. I'm sorry that you ended up in the middle of this mess."

"Jake, I have no regrets. I was the one who volunteered to help the CIA find the terrorists. Nobody twisted my arm. It was solely my decision. I would never have given up the chance of meeting you and getting to know you better, despite the obvious risks. If we hadn't met for coffee in the diner, I might not have reevaluated my life. In the process, I realized I had gotten to the point where I was only going through the motions, doing the same thing over and over and not enjoying it.

This trip has been an opportunity of a lifetime to do something really different that makes a positive impact, and it has been so exciting. I've never felt so alive, but at the same time I've never been truly afraid of anything before. I don't know what I would do if I ever lost you," I said.

As Jake pulled me close, he said, "There's no chance of that. You're stuck with this goofball as long as you'll put up with me."

"Jake, I'm trying to be serious here and talk about our future," I said, trying not to get lost in the heat of the moment, encompassed in his warm yet ever so tender embrace.

Jake said, "I'm sorry, it's just that you're nearly impossible to resist when you're this close. It so happens that I agree with you completely.

I was preoccupied with doing my duty for country. In between, I was trying to drum engineering facts and approaches into these kids at the university while teaching them how to think using logic instead of intuition for a change. Although getting them to realize that their whole life doesn't have to revolve around their little electronic toys is rewarding in itself, I didn't recognize what I was really missing out on until we discovered each other. It's so wonderful to have someone to share everything with. I would never do anything to jeopardize that because I've grown to love you so much."

"I think we found the answer in teaching together at Dana University. Jenni Crowfoot looked so happy talking about her family relationship and teaching her students at the reservation. It made me take a hard look at what my life was all about. I was so envious of what she is doing with her life and the fulfillment she gets from it that I had missed out on. The real question is how can we possibly make it happen for us now?"

"Perhaps Nancy Reagan said it best when she proclaimed the solution to not doing drugs was to just say no. We can stop the CIA work and just start to live our lives like everyone else if and when we get out of here," Jake said. "We can tell Taylor the next time we see her that we've seriously reconsidered her request to continue on with the CIA. Our absolute, final answer will be a resounding no."

"The other thing I was concerned about is being close to you all the time," I said. "Not only at home together but working every day in the same environment. What we have together is wonderful, almost magical, but it's also all so new. Will the magic wear off? Could we grow tired of each other? Are we both too set in our ways to accommodate each other to find a happy medium on everything that will suit us both?"

Jake raised his eyebrows the way he does when he doesn't agree with what he just heard, and said, "Whoa, whoa, whoa, slow down a minute. If you're going to play twenty questions and become wracked with doubt, you'll drive us both crazy. If you start to second guess yourself and us, you'll miss out on all the fantastic joy in life we've both discovered since we found one another. Almost everything we've shared has been too delectable to even contemplate, yet it seems to get better by leaps and bounds with each passing day.

"Don't worry about the future. The element of spontaneity has more than served us well up to this point. Let's just continue to discover each new day together. If I don't say it often enough, thank you for being in my life and putting up with me."

"Maybe you're right. It's just that I love you so much; I'm afraid it will all go poof and evaporate. How was it possible that we were each alone for all those years without finding someone to enjoy life with as much as we do together? What were the chances? Come here and make love with me ever so slowly, all night long," I said as I pulled Jake down on the bed with me.

25

Frenchy picked up Taylor and Manny at the same military airport in Toronto where we had first arrived in Canada and brought them directly out to the Maple Leaf Inn. Gretchen led them to the den where we were waiting with Gord. Frenchy helped her bring in coffee and refreshments before departing, closing the door behind them.

Once we were settled in, Taylor said, "I've got good news and bad news. The good news is that we're still getting useful information out of Singapore and have uncovered yet another plan to detonate several stations of the Underground trains in London simultaneously. Colonel Pickering's people found their cache of C-4, complete with detonators, and they have rounded up all the suspects involved. Furthermore, Major MacNulty has informed us that Canadian Intelligence has everyone involved in the attempt to blow up the Alberta oil fields in custody."

"That's terrific. So what's the bad news? I asked.

"Upon further investigation, we're not sure that all the people involved in Yemen were accounted for," Taylor replied. "That being said, we want to extend an offer to officially bring you both into our witness protection program until we're absolutely certain it is safe for you to resume your original identities."

"What are we supposed to do in the meantime? No offense, Gord, but we don't want to languish in the hinterlands of Canada forever," I said, dismayed because I was starting to develop a severe case of cabin fever.

"None taken," Gord said. "I understand completely."

Taylor said, "We've identified a Suzanne Johnson who had a similar background and professional experience as yours. She graduated from Dana University four years after you did. Suzanne was working for the Fleet Financial Group when she perished in the Twin Towers on 911. It so happens, she was a brunette about your height and weight and didn't have any close relatives."

"So you're proposing I become Suzanne Johnson? What about Jake?" I asked.

"We assumed two new professors starting at Dana University or somewhere else as a couple might draw suspicion, so we figured Jake could continue on as Clifford MacOmber, assuming you both still want to teach this fall," Taylor said.

Jake shook his head when he said, "We thought we would be in the clear to resume our lives together, but this would make it infinitely more complicated. We'll have to talk about it and give it serious thought before we can get back to you."

Manny interjected with, "This is probably a bad time to bring it up, but have you reconsidered the possibility of continuing to support the CIA in any capacity? Please bear in mind that we can be very flexible in accepting whatever terms and conditions that would suit you best."

Jake looked up at Manny and frowned before he replied, "We have discussed the matter at length and have arrived at the decision that we would prefer to sever all ties immediately with the CIA if we get out of our current situation alive. We would also have to contact the deans of the business and engineering schools at DUI to see what we can work out about employment for the fall semester, since we can't show up as Jacob Wells and Pamela Mullen. Obviously, we would have to tell them on a confidential basis that we would need to be new hires as Suzanne Johnson and Clifford MacOmber." Taylor said, "After all you've both done for the CIA to identify the people determined to cause death and destruction in the United States, we have no plans to abandon you. We will expedite precursory background checks on both deans and work out a way to coordinate a confidential meeting with them. In the meantime, since you indicated you've had preliminary discussions with the dean of the DU Business School, you'll have to contact her right away to put a temporary hold on your request for employment before Pamela Mullen's appointment is announced."

"How much longer will we need to stay here at the inn?" I asked.

Taylor said, "Because you have no ties to the area, we doubt anyone would ever think of looking for Jake or you in Canada. We suspect we can have answers to all of your questions in another week's time. In the meantime, please continue to have Major MacNulty channel all your outside communications between Canadian Intelligence and the CIA."

26

In spite of being consumed with overwhelming trepidation about what might happen if our plans to teach at Dana University together were not realized, the week seemed to fly by. Perhaps it was due to the sense of community or the degree of mutual comfort and affection we had developed over time with Gord, Gretchen, and Frenchy.

Taylor and Manny once again returned to the inn for the express purpose of providing us with a detailed status review of the terrorists in captivity, intelligence gathered, and options for our future. Getting right down to business, Manny informed us that the CIA had thoroughly reexamined the interrogation transcripts of the prisoners relocated to the Guantanamo Bay Detention Camp combined with detailed financial forensics of the money transfers, e-mails, wire taps, and telephone records. Based on their findings, the CIA was convinced they had rounded up all the participants in the United States and Britain involved in the plot to poison the water supply of the greater Boston area.

The CIA initially thought that only the leader of the plan to poison the Quabbin Reservoir might have escaped the Yemen drone attacks, but further DNA testing on all the body parts gathered at the site reveled he was at the center of the direct hit on the compound. They did locate a sufficient number of diverse parts to confirm he couldn't have escaped the blast, leading them to the conclusion that there were no survivors after the attack by the drone missiles.

Taylor then told us that they still could find no evidence that my involvement was known about, including my contributions to tracking down and identifying the terrorists. Since the few remaining prisoners who knew about Jake would be held incommunicado indefinitely; the CIA felt it would be safe for Jake and I to resume our lives as civilians. As previously explained by Taylor and Manny, the CIA still felt it might be wise for us to have unrelated backgrounds if we plan to start new careers as Suzanne Johnson and Clifford MacOmber at Dana University or more preferably, at different institutions. Since Jake already had all the necessary paperwork as Cliff, I was presented with photo identification and a biography as Suzanne Johnson to commit to memory.

Even though the Islamic plans to poison millions of innocent people in Massachusetts were derailed, Jake's life could still be in jeopardy, much like the fatwa bounty declared in Iran resulted in the author Sir Salman Rushdie having to remain in hiding for eight years.

The CIA thought the chances were too great that many former students and colleagues might recognize Jake at Dana University, even with a full beard, mustache, and a longer hair style. Manny had the other major schools in the area researched and found an opening for a professor of chemical engineering at the University of Massachusetts in Amherst. Manny had arranged a confidential interview meeting with the UMass dean of engineering, John Perry, to discuss the possibility of Clifford MacOmber coming on board as a new hire for the fall semester. He would be the only one to know it was Jacob Wells. Although Jake wouldn't be together with me at the same school, the commute would not be that far.

After a security clearance check on the background of Dean Brytowski was expedited, Taylor had contacted her to explain my situation. The dean was concerned that Pamela Mullen had backed out of her agreement to fill the vacancy in the Dana University School of Business. She was at once elated, anxious, and accommodating to accept me under the name of Suzanne Johnson as a replacement. She did request assurance that the CIA would provide adequate back-up documentation for Dr. Johnson, so no one would think to question my qualifications for the position.

Manny had arranged for the interview meeting with the dean of engineering at the University of Massachusetts to be held in a conference room at the Hampton Inn the following Tuesday. Part of the purpose of the CIA's involvement was to review the ground rules to assure the confidentiality and safety of Jake as Cliff. Manny had made arrangements for a military reconnaissance plane to take us into Barnes Airport in Westfield for the interview.

Because I was so excited that I finally could see the light at the end of the tunnel relative to being able to really start the next chapter of my life with Jake, it was all I could do to refrain from jumping up and down with joy. Not being able to contain myself any longer, I gave Manny a big kiss and a hug, before turning to Jake and doing the same to him.

When I released a surprised Jake at last, I turned back to Manny who looked like he was still in shock. As I said, "Oh, thank you, thank you!" Manny assumed a both hands up, palms out in front of him defensive posture, as if to prevent me from assaulting him a second time.

Basking in our joy that she and Manny had been able to help repay us for our assistance in locating and thwarting the terrorists' efforts to create mayhem and fear, Taylor acted reserved, but she positively beamed. She said they would meet us at Barnes when we touched down to provide security and to help explain the reasons to Dean Perry why Jake needed to work as Clifford MacOmber.

We said good-bye to Manny and Taylor before they departed with Frenchy for the Toronto airport. I felt sad knowing that after next Tuesday, we might not see them again. It was surprising that we could have grown so close, working together for such a short period of time.

I had never known time to drag so slowly as it did before the magical day of Tuesday arrived at last. It felt like it was a milestone or maybe a steppingstone for Jake, Cliff, Suzanne, and me to start our new lives together. I had to stop and ask myself if I might be going crazy when it had started to seem normal for both of us to have two names—or three, in my case. At least I would have Brenda and Suzanne to talk to when Jake and Cliff weren't around. Then I would no longer need to talk to myself.

Gord and Gretchen came with us to the airport with Frenchy for protection and to see us off. When they dropped us at the military, two propeller observation plane, Gretchen and I both were close to tears at our parting. The guys didn't look any too happy about parting ways either, since we had all become sort of a tight-knit family. We hugged and shook hands, promising we'd try to get back together someday, if that were possible down the road.

Once we were on board the plane, the only extra things we had to wear on this trip were headphones to be able to talk to each other and to protect our hearing from the engine noise. At least Jake and I were together for this flight. The sky was gray and overcast, which kind of matched our mood because we had to say farewell to our Canadian friends. Once we were airborne and enclosed by the clouds, the pilot had to rely on instruments because visibility was so poor at cruising altitude.

Over the headphones, Jake asked the pilot, "What is the stall speed of this thing?"

"It's 180 knots; why do you ask?" the pilot responded.

Jake said, "It's been so long since I flew on something other than a jet. I needed to know at what speed I should get out and push to keep the nose straight and level."

The pilot responded with a big grin, "I understand you were an army ranger. We could fly over the field and let you parachute down when we get there."

Jake threw his hands up in the air and said, "Okay, Okay, I'll stop making fun of your equipment, because I've never done a parachute drop with my luggage in hand. I have flown on worse though."

After three hours of a little turbulence and a few air pockets with sudden drops, we broke through the clouds descending between the spots of sunbeams peeking through the holes in the clouds over the Berkshire Mountains. The crops of different colors in the hilly fields below made it look like a continuous series of checkerboards. At least we wouldn't need to rely on instruments for the landing below the cloud cover.

Following an exceptionally smooth landing, Jake gave the pilot a big thumbs up sign with a broad smile. As we neared the end of the runway, we saw Taylor and Manny were waiting for us in front of the hangar next to their government issue big, black SUV. Because we were in our disguises, the plane could stop outside the hangar this time.

I was so elated that this could be our first major step of our return to some sense of normalcy in our lives; I reached over to squeeze Jake's arm. He smiled and put his big hand over mine.

Upon deplaning and grabbing our luggage, we stowed the bags in the back of the car and greeted our CIA agents.

Jake hopped in the front with Manny, and I got in the back with Taylor.

Since we were a little ahead of schedule, Manny suggested we stop for coffee at the Dunkin Donuts on Route 9 in Northampton. After almost a month of being squirreled away in a safe house, this was kind of a treat for us. Jake settled for an old-fashioned, plain donut with his coffee. Not for me. I had to have a Boston cream-filled donut with thick chocolate frosting slathered over the top. If I had to eat all those calories, I was going to thoroughly enjoy it. Fortunately, they had plenty of napkins.

We still had enough time to reach the Hampton Inn for our appointment with John Perry. Manny had spoken with the dean on the telephone about the position and why the meeting had to be confidential, but it was obvious that Dean Perry was surprised to see four of us show up for the interview. We were ushered to a suite on the top floor where Manny and Taylor explained to him that we had to go into hiding after we finish our undercover assignments for the CIA. He was permitted to inquire what Cliff's experience was in detail, just not at what school.

Jake (as Cliff MacOmber) went into a separate room with Dean Perry for the interview while I remained in the central room of the suite with Taylor and Manny. They explained to me that if all went well with the interview, the CIA would keep track of us with our new identities on both campuses for a few weeks until they were confident we were no longer in danger.

Jake and John emerged from the interview smiling. John shook his hand and said, "Welcome aboard, Cliff. I look forward to seeing you on campus."

After John left the suite, Manny said, "We could stop to eat somewhere, but after all you've been through, we suspect you'd like to get back to your house to enjoy a little peace and quiet together."

On the way out to the car, Manny said, "We took the liberty to restock your refrigerator and freezer with food."

When Jake said, "How did you get in…never mind, forget I asked." This provoked grins from both Taylor and Manny.

Arriving at Jake's place, Taylor said, "Thank you for all your help and patience with us. Please don't worry; we still have your backs. We'll leave to let you have some well deserved time alone."

With that, we dragged our bags through the door. I looked up at Jake and said, "There's no place like home! Now get that silly fuzz off your face, so I can have my way with you."

27

"Jake, Jake, wake up! I heard a noise outside," I said, shaking Jake's shoulder.

"Huh? What kind of noise?

"It was a loud crack, like a stick breaking."

"It was probably just a bear or a deer. We are out in the country. Maybe it was an overweight owl landing on a dead tree limb. Go back to sleep. Manny said the CIA will be keeping an eye on the place."

"Jake, what if they didn't get all the terrorists? What if they found out where your house is?"

"Pam, I have a post office box mailing address. You're the only one who has been out here since I moved in. I have direct deposit and all my bills are paid automatically. The people I worked with don't even know where I live. Can we get back to sleep now?"

"Please go check so I can relax. I haven't been able to calm my nerves down since we were attacked in London."

"Okay, if it's the only way we can both return to dreamland. I'll go down to the garage to get my spare gun from the toolbox," Jake said as he rolled out of bed and lifted the slats on the Venetian blinds to peek out each of the bedroom windows. "I don't see anything outside."

"Jake, I'm not staying here by myself. I'm coming with you."

"All right, if you stay behind me in case there is really someone out there. Why don't you give me that penlight from your pocketbook so we don't trip over anything in the dark?"

Jake took my hand as he tiptoed through the kitchen. "Try to be very quiet," he whispered over his shoulder while slowly turning the knob on the door to the garage.

"Ouch," he mumbled half aloud as he stepped barefoot on a bolt on the floor next to the workbench. Letting go of my hand, he used both hands to carefully open each latch and lift the lid of the toolbox to avoid making noise. Removing the gun from the tray, he flipped the safety off, and took my hand once again to lead me back to the kitchen in the dark.

Hearing the sound of glass breaking coming from the living room, Jake whispered, "Stay here," as he crept to the doorway just in time to see an arm reaching through the broken window to turn the deadbolt. As the door opened, Jake yelled at the shadowy figure, "Put your hands up where I can see them!"

Seeing the mysterious intruder start to raise one arm with a gun, Jake fired off three rounds on reflex. As the man dropped, I rushed into the living room saying, "Jake, are you all right?"

"Pam, I'm okay, stay back," he said pushing me away.

He approached the body and kicked the gun out of reach. Jake leaned down and shook his head to indicate there was no sign of a pulse over the carotid artery. Just then Jake looked up because he must have realized a number of high intensity flashlights were rushing toward the house from several directions. Flipping the floodlight switch, Jake saw the people running at him wore flak jackets imprinted with CIA in large letters.

He put down his gun, raised both hands, and stepped around the body and broken glass to greet them outside. "Where were you when I needed you?" Jake said.

A booming voice from the right said, "Cliff MacOmber I presume? Do you have any ID?"

"Not in my pajamas," Jake replied. "Where's yours?"

"I'm Special Agent Robert Maxwell," he answered, holding up his photo ID and badge for examination.

"Come inside, so I can check on Suzanne. How did the bad guy get past all of you?" Jake asked.

"We don't know, we had the place surrounded."

Fortunately, Suzanne's hearing must be better than yours then," Jake said as he stepped around the body on the way in.

"Oh, Cliff, thank heavens you're still in one piece," I said rushing to Jake's side.

Hitting a speed dial number on his cell phone, Maxwell said, "I'll see if I can get in touch with agents Rodriquez or Young… Manny, Bob here. Sorry to wake you. We've had an incident… A gunman got as far as the house… No, they're both okay. MacOmber shot the intruder… We're searching the grounds to see if there's anyone else or a vehicle… We'll get back to you when we have more information… Goodbye."

Jake sat at the kitchen table with Bob to discuss all the details of what happened while I put on a pot of coffee. By the time everything was documented, photographed, and the body taken away, Taylor and Manny showed up a little after sunrise.

"What can I say? We thought we had all the bases covered. I'm sorry. I'm just happy that you're both okay. So much for the best laid plans of mice and men," Taylor said.

"We've initiated action to get you back into our relocation program," Manny said.

"It doesn't seem as though we're safe anywhere in this area, and I have had my fill of safe houses," I said. "I want to be able to lead a normal life without looking over my shoulder. It seems that the only one I can rely on for my protection is Jake, and that's good enough for me. I have a sufficient amount of money set aside that we can afford to take a year off and travel while we decide what we want to do. The only thing that matters is that we're together. We don't want anyone to know where we are."

"Is that how you feel too, Jake?" Manny asked.

"What she just said," Jake replied. "We want to be left alone to be together. The CIA can arrange to store the stuff in my house and Pam's apartment. We will sign power of attorney papers for you to sell both places and our vehicles. Please put the money in an interest-bearing account for us. You can also contact both universities for us with our regrets and apologies. In the meantime, we will ride off into the sunset and contact you in a year or so. We need to do our own thing to reclaim our lives and sanity."

"Are you absolutely sure about this?" Taylor asked. "We've never been more certain of anything," I said. "We have each other, and that's all we need. Now if you excuse us long enough to pack, you can arrange to get us to the airport where we plan to magically disappear."

www.ingramcontent.com/pod-product-compliance
Lightning Source LLC
LaVergne TN
LVHW021714060526
838200LV00050B/2650
9781643676586